ONE
WEEKEND

Darby West

1ST J

That Special Touch, Ink

Also by Darby West
Through the Fire

The Monkey & the Crocodile

Today I Kissed a Butterfly Hello

Maribeth!

Trying to Breathe Under Water

First Edition

Cover Designed by: Sharon Blount

ISBN: 978-0-9790200-6-3

DEDICATION

KB

1

I MET MARC IN THE SUMMER of 1976. We had both graduated from high school and our families had taken us out to eat dinner at Beefsteak Charlie's in Manhattan to celebrate. As soon as we were seated, I saw him. He met my gaze and smiled. His hair was in cornrows all going back, showing off his perfect forehead. His smile seemed to light up the entire room.

There had to be at least twenty people sitting at the tables that were pushed together for his family. I could see from where I sat at the table with my family that he was just as bored as I was with the excitement our families were showing.

He mouthed the words, "Meet me outside!" I looked behind me to make sure he was referring to me. Marc was tall and skinny then, he had a few acne bumps on his face, and a few sprigs of hair coming in above his top lip. He sat there grinning, showing big white teeth, and mouthed it again. I told my mother I was going to the restroom and instead went outside where Marc was now waiting for me on the corner.

"Hi there," he said, still grinning. His graduation cap now sat precariously on his head. His braids lay on his shoulders. "Hi! So, let me guess, your parents forced you to share your day with your entire family?" I teased him. "Yes! Just like your parents did you!" he said laughing.

"What's your name?" he asked.

"Dedra, but everyone calls me DeeDee," I replied.

"Where did you graduate?"

"Erasmus Hall. What about you?" I asked.

"Brooklyn Tech," he said, and popped his collar proudly.

I liked his cockiness back then as a teenager who had probably been told by his parents that he was the greatest. He was a popular basketball player, football, and baseball player, and was also on the honor roll. He had gotten a scholarship to attend Howard University in Washington, DC. He said it with so much pride, I was almost embarrassed to tell him that I was going to be attending Fordham University. I expected he would make light of my school.

"That's cool! Congratulations," he said surprising me.

We exchanged phone numbers and I wondered if he would truly call me.

"I've got to get back inside," I told him.

We went back into the restaurant and joined our families, who didn't even seem to have missed us.

That summer we hung out together, going to Coney Island on the weekend and to Yankee Stadium each time his dad got him tickets to catch a ball game. We promised that we would stay in touch when he left to go to college. At first, Marc and I did stay in touch, but we both had so much going on, that soon our phone calls were sporadic, and eventually, we just stopped talking. I was busy with class, and he was busy with class, as well.

His call caught me totally off guard, but I was glad to hear from him. It had been nearly three years since we had last spoken. He wanted to know if he could come by and visit that Saturday at three. He called at the perfect time because I was not seeing anyone.

I was braiding my mom's hair when he rang the buzzer to get into our building. I looked at the clock on the wall and it was just a little before two! He was early; very early. I let him into the building and Mommie said she could wait to get her hair braided until he left. She put a scarf on her head, and we waited for him to come up the stairs. Marc had changed in the time since I had last seen him. He was no longer the skinny kid he was when he left to go to DC. He wore his hair in a nice cut and had grown a full mustache. His acne had cleared up, and he looked very handsome.

I fixed him something to drink and we sat in the living room talking. He told me that things were going well for him in DC, but he missed New York. He had hoped to start a job in the finance district in Manhattan in a few months when he graduated.

I was happy for him and told him about my big plans as well. I was going to be working on Wall Street, at a prestigious law firm. This time I had something to brag about, but I chose not to.

I asked him what made him call me after all of this time. He got up and came to sit beside me and reached for my hand. For a split second, I thought he was about to get on one knee.

He didn't say anything at first, he just kept looking at my hand in his. Finally, he spoke.

"I couldn't stop thinking about you. I've met a couple of women since I was in DC. But, you were always on my mind. I told myself, I had to come back and see if I could get you again. So, here I am," he said.

From the kitchen, where my mother was eavesdropping, I heard her say, "Awwww!"

We both laughed at her. That's how we got back together and began dating again.

A few months after I graduated, I moved into an apartment with my best friend Joyce, in Crown Heights, Brooklyn.

Joyce and I had been friends since elementary school. We had always talked about living together when we grew up and got jobs. So, no one was surprised when we moved into Joyce's deceased grandmother's rent-controlled apartment.

Joyce and I had so much in common physically, that people that didn't know us, thought we were sisters. We both liked big hair and braids. When we weren't sporting braids with beads, we wore huge Afros. Both of us liked African clothing, and a boho look. Though Joyce was slimmer than me, we often shared clothing.

Joyce was dating a few guys, but no one serious. That was one thing that was different about us. I just had room in my life for one guy at a time. However, it worked for her and I didn't knock it.

2

MARC AND I HAD BEEN engaged for eleven months when he decided he wanted to join the U. S. Air Force. Things were not going as well as he wanted them to at his job, and he felt that he could return to school using the GI bill. I had a good job working as a secretary at a law firm in lower Manhattan, and I enjoyed my job. Therefore, I wasn't too excited about leaving New York. Even though I didn't want to leave New York, I didn't try talking him out of it since he seemed adamant about joining the military.

Finally, he joined the Air Force and was sent to San Antonio, Texas for six weeks of basic training. I continued working and dreading when I would have to join him wherever he was going to be sent. I prayed it wasn't going to be in another country.

Meanwhile, Joyce and I were spending as much time as we could together. One night after a Teddy Pendergrass concert, we went back to our apartment, carrying flasks filled with Hennessy and a take-out order of fried chicken wings and fries.

I put on my pajamas and got comfortable on the sofa.

"What am I going to do without you here, Dee Dee? Who is going to put up with me? You know I can't stand none of these chicks we hang out with!" she said, pretending to be crying.

"I'll come back often to see you. And you know you can come and visit me!" I said, taking a big swig of my drink.

"You promise?" We hugged quickly, bumping our heads together accidentally.

I was going to miss her; however, I knew we were going to always be friends, and no amount of miles would be able to separate us.

Marc finished basic training but failed to mention that he also had eight weeks of technical school for him to be an engineer. It didn't seem like we were ever going to be together. In basic training, we couldn't even talk on the telephone. At least now we could talk, and he called me every Sunday afternoon. Finally, that was over, and he flew to New York to see his family and me. He had good news – he was going to be stationed in Alamogordo, New Mexico! I was so afraid he was going to say some foreign country.

A few days after he came home, our immediate family and Joyce gathered with us at the courthouse, where we got married before a justice of the peace.

The morning Marc and I got on the road heading out to New Mexico in my red Volkswagen Beetle the sun was just coming up. We stopped by Dad's apartment building to get the gift he had for me. I ran up to his apartment and gently knocked on his door. He had gotten up and made my favorite breakfast biscuit: sausage, egg, and cheese. He handed me a Tupperware container with piping hot sausage biscuits and walked me out to the car. Marc got out, hugged Daddy, and promised he would take good care of me. Daddy walked around to the driver's door and slipped some money into my hand.

"Call me when you get there," he said, wiping the tears from his eyes.

"I will, Daddy. Don't cry. I'll be back to visit soon," I promised.

While driving, I gave the container to Marc to hold. "Hand me a biscuit, please."

I was going to miss New York. As I drove away, I kept glancing into the rearview mirror. After Marc had eaten a couple of biscuits, he did what he always did after eating – he went to sleep. He didn't wake up until we had gotten to Ohio.

We ate dinner and hit the road again. This time, Marc drove for a couple of hours before he got tired again, and we got a hotel for the night.

After taking a shower, I called my dad to let him know where we were. Then I called Joyce. The whole time we talked, Marc lay beside me, snoring loudly.

"Did he do all the driving?" Joyce asked.

"Girl, please. The man slept all the way to Ohio and then drove just two hours before he got tired. We're leaving out of here around six in the morning. I want to try to at least get to Oklahoma before nightfall. If I do, I do. If not, I am pulling off to get a room again."

"You have a good night. I love you."

"I love you more."

I was tired, and my feet were restless from all the driving, but I finally fell asleep. When the alarm rang the next morning, I was ready to hit the road.

Once again, I took the first leg of driving, promising myself this time, I was only going to drive for three hours and let Marc take the wheel. However, it didn't go as planned. When I stopped that morning at a McDonald's, I went in to use the bathroom and get some biscuits.

When I returned to the car, Marc was still snoring and refused to wake up. I drove on for a couple of more hours, and finally, I pulled into a rest stop and waited for him to wake up. I was tired, too. I had no place I had to be at a certain time; he did. He got sick of me fussing and took the wheel for the next five hours. I curled up in the backseat, sleeping well.

When I woke up, we were in Texas.

3

WE STOPPED IN A SMALL town in Texas called Powhite and got something to eat. Neither of us had ever heard of it, nor were we sure how to pronounce it. So, based solely on the spelling and how we chose to pronounce it, we got our food to go. I took over driving and ate as I drove. At nine that evening, I stopped at another hotel, and we spent the night. I took a hot shower, too tired to do anything but wrap the towel around me and go to bed. When the alarm rang the next morning, we hit the road again. He slept as I drove us to Alamogordo. After driving nonstop for four more hours, we were finally at our destination.

My red Volkswagen was covered in dust and dirt, but we were finally there.

A few days later, we moved into a fully furnished double wide mobile home in a trailer park with rows and rows of single-wide trailers. Our trailer stuck out like a sore thumb. The only reason we took that one, was because it was the last one available. While Marc was at work, I was getting to know my neighbors.

The movers arrived the same day we moved into the mobile home.

When someone rang the doorbell, I was unpacking some boxes that were marked "Kitchen." I went to the door to see an African American man standing there. He still had on his uniform; his cap turned backward on his head. He looked a bit unkempt, sporting a close beard, and grease stains on his uniform. He was smiling, showing beautiful white teeth and a dimple in just one cheek. I could tell he worked outside because of his sun-kissed complexion and the red tint that showed signs of sunburn.

"Hey! How are you? I'm your neighbor from right over there. I just came to welcome you to the block!" he said cheerfully. I opened the door and stepped onto the porch. "I'm Wayne." His smile was contagious.

"Hi, Wayne, nice to meet you. I'm Dedra. Everyone calls me Dee Dee. Are you from New York?" I asked, detecting his accent.

"You can tell? Yeah, I'm from Queens. Where are you from?"

"Brooklyn."

"Yeah? Where in Brooklyn? I have family there!"

"Crown Heights."

"I know that area very well. My cousins live there."

Wayne's wife was visiting family in New York, so I didn't meet Sherita that day.

"Have you gotten the tour of the city?" he asked.

"Not yet."

"I was going downtown to grab a bite. Do you want to come with me? I can give you a quick tour. I'm safe." He added, "If your husband doesn't mind."

I went back inside to change pants and get my shoes and some money. I honestly didn't even think Marc would be upset I had gone downtown with Wayne. I scribbled a note and left it on the fridge for Marc. I followed Wayne to his beat-up Chevy pickup truck. It was up so high, I couldn't get in. "Grab the handle up there, and pull yourself in," he instructed. But that wasn't working. Laughing, he got out and came around to help me get in. It seemed the only way to push me up into the truck was to touch my butt, but he didn't want to do that. So, he turned his back and pushed me up that way. It was at least 110 degrees that day, but he had no air conditioner. The hot dry air was a beast!

As we rode toward downtown, he began pointing out attractions we might be interested in visiting.

"If you like Mexican food, this is the joint that has the best tacos in the city," he said, pulling into the parking lot of a rundown looking building. The sign in the window simply said, "Tacos." I had to admit I had never had Mexican food before. So, naturally, they were the best tacos I had ever eaten!

After we left there, we drove up to the mountains. He showed me where there was a stocked trout pond, a natural spring to get fresh water, and a country store that sold items made from fresh apples, berries, and pears.

When we finally returned, Marc was home, sitting on the porch, looking a bit disturbed. When he had left for work that morning, he had said he would be gone most of the day due to training. Wayne stopped in front of our mobile home to let me out and drove on to his place two doors down. Then he came over to meet Marc.

"Hey, man! What's up? I'm Wayne," he said, holding out his hand. Marc shook his hand and stated his name; however, I could tell he was agitated.

"I gave your wife a shortened tour of the city. Would you like to get one?"

"Naw, that's okay. I'm good."

Wayne could see that Marc was upset, so he thanked me for going with him and went back home. With Marc right on my heels, I went inside our home. He followed me to the kitchen, where I put the gallon containers of homemade apple juice I had purchased in the refrigerator.

"Who the hell is that?" he asked.

"That's Wayne! Didn't you hear him?" I asked.

"You had me worried. I didn't know what had happened to you." "I left you a note on the fridge."

"I saw that, but I couldn't figure out who the heck Wayne was. We just got here two days ago, and already you know folks?"

"Yes, I know folks. I get out and mingle. I got you some tacos. Would you like them for your dinner?"

"Do you hear me talking to you? You didn't even know this guy, and you jump in the car and go all over the city with him. I could have shown you around on my day off."

"Could you keep your voice down? He'll hear you."

"I don't care if he hears me!"

I went down the hall to our bedroom, so Wayne would not hear him ranting like a fool. I knew he wasn't trying to act like he was jealous of me! I took off my shoes and put them back in the closet with him following me from one room to another. I went to the bathroom with him still fussing because I had gone downtown with Wayne.

"Okay! I met him; he seemed cool. I didn't see the danger, so you're right, okay. Now can we please change the subject? I got you some tacos!" I said, holding the bag out to him. He snatched it and went back to our bedroom, pouting like a little kid!

The next day when I saw Wayne, I apologized for Marc's rude behavior.

"No problem. I understand where he was coming from. You're fine, you're his wife, and he doesn't know me from Jack. So, I understand, and I would probably have done the same thing. It's all good. You want to go to the zoo?" he asked.

"Let me get my shoes!" I said, laughing.

Wayne and I went back downtown, stopped at the taco joint, and then went to the zoo.

"How long have you been married?" he asked.

"Three weeks."

"Oh! No wonder your man is tripping! I've been married for two years. I married a girl from my neighborhood. She's different," he said, looking away, stifling a smile.

"What? What do you mean she's different? She's a woman, isn't she?"

"Yeah, she's a woman! She keeps me on my toes. She likes to argue. She likes to fight. She doesn't like too many people. I don't even think she likes my mom or my sisters. She's one of those folks that either likes you or she doesn't. If she doesn't, she thinks it's her mission to make your life miserable."

"Wow! I'm not sure I want to meet her."

"I think she'll like you."

18

"Why?"

"I just do! Anyway, she's coming back home next Wednesday. I have to pick her up from the airport," he said, smiling this time.

On Wednesday, when someone rang the doorbell, I was taking clothes out of the dryer. I went to the door to see Sherita. She wasn't smiling, but her voice was pleasant. Sherita was light skinned and had freckles on her nose and cheeks. Her hair was a sandy blond color and her eyes were gray with little flecks of brown in them.

"I'm Sherita, Wayne's wife. He told me to come over and meet you." The way Sherita said it was as if she didn't want to; she only came because he had insisted she come.

I opened the door to let her inside. She stepped in and stood there. "Come on in, have a seat," I said, motioning toward the sofa.

"I'm not going to be here very long."

Her face was frowned as she looked around the room.

"Have you met any of our other neighbors?"

"Yes. I've met the lady in the mobile home in front of yours, the lady over there, and one behind me. Everyone is very friendly."

"Humpf!"

I didn't know what that sound meant. I had a bunch of stuff to do, so I hoped she wasn't going to give me the rundown on each of the neighbors I said I had met. Sherita sat down on the sofa, right at the edge, as if she was going to get up and leave any minute.

"How long have you been married?" she asked.

"We've only been married four weeks, what about you?" I asked.

"Oh, you mean Wayne left that out? I heard that you two have been going to the park and zoo, hanging out, and eating lunch together," she said in an accusatory tone. I didn't like her! Wayne was right; she was obnoxious.

"He may have told me, and I just forgot," I said, trying hard to sound pleasant. I looked at the clock, and she followed my gaze.

"Oh, you have something to do? I'll be going. As I said, Wayne told me to come over and meet you. So, we've met." For the first time since entering the house, she smiled. It looked so out of place on her frowned face.

I walked Sherita to the door and closed it behind her gently. "Wow!" I said.

That evening when Marc came home, I told him about her visit. "Well, what did you expect? You were hanging out with her husband while she was out of town! If I were a jealous man, I would feel the same way as she does!" he said.

"You were acting just like a jealous man when you met Wayne. What are you saying?" I asked, laughing

He didn't think it was funny, so I let it go.

A few days later, Marc and I went downtown. I showed him some of the places Wayne had shown me. We also went up to the mountains. I knew about the stock pond place. Fishers paid the owners $2.00, and then they would let them fish in the pond. I didn't know that each fish we caught had to be paid for by the inch. We each had two big fish. When the man rang up the sale and announced we owed him $60 for those four fish, I wanted to throw mine back in the pond.

"Do you know how many fish we could have gotten from the fish market with $60?" Marc asked, putting the fish in the cooler. I agreed with him. It was ridiculous! I didn't even want to eat my fish right away. I wanted to have it stuffed and put on the wall.

Instead, we cleaned them, and I fried them for dinner. I ate mine slowly, savoring every single morsel. From now on, we would get our fish from the fish market downtown next to the taco shop.

4

EACH DAY, MARC WOULD go to work, and I would be stuck at home with nothing to do. We only had one car, which was mine, and I felt like it was time for him to get a car, even if it were a jalopy. I needed my car during the day so that I could go places. Besides, I wanted to get a job.

Marc finally purchased a beat-up old Ford Pinto to get back and forth to work. I went downtown to the employment office and enrolled with them. Since I had to quit my job because my husband joined the military, I was eligible for unemployment. As I was leaving the office, I saw a sign on the wall for taking a course in bartending. I wasn't doing anything, so I decided to register for the class. It was only an eight-week course for four hours a day.

I enjoyed the class and decided to apply for a job at both of the clubs: the Non-Commissioned Officers' Club and the Officers' Club.

I didn't know which one would call me first. Whichever one called first, I was taking the job.

It just so happened that the Officers' Club called first. After the interview with the club manager, he handed me a pen and several forms to fill out, and I was hired. The other bartender was a tall Native American woman named Lisa. Without even telling me she was Native American, I knew. She had high cheekbones and wore her jet-black hair in a pony-tail that hung past her ample behind. Lisa had been working there for nearly seventeen years. She had been there so long, she could fix a drink with her eyes closed.

She and I got along well together and decided we both didn't need to work during the week at the same time, so we alternated nights. Friday and Saturday nights were our busiest time; we both worked on those two nights. Four cocktail waitresses assisted us.

Marc decided we should move on the base and applied for housing. They told us we should hear something in about six months or less. We both hated the drive to the base and was glad when we got called for housing sooner.

Another reason I was glad was that everyone I had met in the trailer park was now living on the base.

The duplex apartment we got was a hop and skip away from the club. If I wanted to, I could have walked to work. It was also more convenient for Marc. He was enjoying his job, and I was enjoying mine, especially the tips.

One thing my father taught me was never to tell all of your business when it comes to money. So, I opened a separate bank account, and that is where I deposited all of my tip money. Sometimes I would have a tip jar with over $400 in it at the end of a weekend shift.

Seven months after we got married, I missed a period and immediately knew I was pregnant. I had never missed a period before in my life. When I told Marc, he was more excited than I was. I had thought we would wait a year or two before getting pregnant. That would give us a chance to get to know each other better as man and wife. I was already finding out things about him that I didn't know before.

One of them was how much he flirted with women. I wasn't jealous, but sometimes it seemed he was flirting with women right in front of me to see if I would say anything about it.

As the months of my pregnancy went by, Marc went with me to my doctor's appointments. He rubbed my feet and my back as the baby grew. I knew, eventually, I would have to take leave from work since I was getting big, and I was always tired.

One cold December day, I went into labor while Marc was at work. I called his job and told them to tell him to meet me at the hospital; my water had broken. I drove myself there. The nurse helped me get into a gown. When Marc came in with his green scrubs on, she was just about to hook me up to the monitor. I had hoped he would be able to be there. I wasn't planning on doing this again anytime soon!

When our little girl was born twenty minutes later, we both cried tears of joy. After I was in the room, I called my dad to tell him, and Marc called his family to tell them. We were so happy. Since the baby came a couple of weeks early, we hadn't even put the crib together or got the nursery set up as I wanted it. When we came home three days later, the baby, who we named Jazmine, slept in the bassinet I had gotten at a yard sale. It had never been used and was gorgeous. The owner said she had gotten it in Germany, and thought she was having a girl, but ended up having a little boy. She didn't want to put him in a pink bassinet.

During the day when the baby was sleeping, I started putting together her crib. I had asked Marc to do it, but he was a procrastinator. I just went ahead and did it. When he came home from work one evening, it was put together and I had finished decorating the nursery.

Marc seemed to be preoccupied and said work was stressing him out. Some of the guys in his unit, from when he first came here, seemed to be getting orders to leave. Every weekend, there was a going-away party for someone in his unit. He would get dressed up, smelling good, and would leave to wish someone well at their next base. "None of these guys are married?" I asked him one evening as he was getting dressed to go to yet, another going away party for one of his co-workers. I thought it odd that just the fellows got together and not the family.

"No. They are all single guys. But, I will let you know when it's a couple," he said. I locked the door after he left and came to the bedroom. I was watching TV and must have dozed off for a few minutes. I didn't like the baby sleeping in the bed with me, so I went to her room to turn back the covers in her crib so I could lay her down.

When the telephone rang, I was returning to our bedroom after putting Jazmine back into her crib.

I glanced at the clock, seeing it was nearly three in the morning. Marc hadn't gotten home yet. I didn't know if something had happened to him, and he was calling. I quickly picked it up, so it didn't wake up the baby.

"Marc, where are you?" I asked, assuming it was him.

"This isn't Marc, but he is on his way home. We had a great time tonight," a woman said and hung up.

This wasn't the first time this chick had called me, either. However, it was the first time she had called at this hour. When I asked Marc about the first few calls, he tried to act surprised and blew it off as a kid playing on the phone, but I knew it wasn't a kid calling. This was a grown woman, and she was having an affair with my husband! I knew he would deny it when he did get home, so I didn't even bother to tell him about it. Instead, I got under the covers and went back to sleep. I was sick of his flirting behind, anyway.

We couldn't even go to the supermarket together without him stopping to flirt with the cashier, or the bagger, or even a woman in the parking lot, who was putting her groceries in her trunk!

We were always arguing about his flirting. He was always assuring me that he was just flirting. "You're married!" I would shout at him.

After my six-week examination, I decided to go back to work to get out of the house. I missed the folks I worked with and the money. Mainly the money! Since Marc worked during the day, he could watch the baby at night. I wouldn't have to pay for a sitter.

Things were going pretty well with our arrangements until he decided she was preventing him from hanging out with his friends. Now I had to find a babysitter. Sherita was on the base, but she wasn't a babysitter. "Let me check and see if my friend, Gloria, can watch her for you. I'll call you back," she said.

Gloria agreed to watch Jazmine. Sherita and I went by her duplex so I could meet her. Gloria's husband worked with Wayne. They had one little four-year-old boy. Her home was spotless, and she was nice. She only charged me $40 a week to watch the baby.

Now when I got off in the wee hours of the morning, I had to go to Gloria's house, wake her up, and get my daughter when her father was lying right there sleeping in bed some nights. If he wasn't home when I got off at two or three in the morning, I knew he was either going to call and lie that he had too much to drink and was going to crash on his "friend's" sofa or he wouldn't even call at all. His mistress kept me up to date on what was going on with him. I wasn't even sure if he was aware I could report him to his CO, and the Air Force would throw him out on his backside! *Let him keep playing with me!*

5

IT HAD BEEN A LONG WEEK at work at the officer's club. Two of the cocktail waitresses had quit. Their husbands had gotten orders to go to a new base. Though the manager was interviewing replacements, he hadn't found anyone yet. As a result, Lisa and I had to tend to the bar and act as the waitress. My feet were killing me by the time I got home each night. I didn't want my sleep disturbed by a woman telling me she was sleeping with that sorry husband of mine.

The next night at work, everything that could happen had happened. The ice machine stopped working mid-shift. I had to get a bucket and get ice from the kitchen's icemaker and carry it back to the club. The dishwasher also stopped working. No one had informed me; I arrived at my shift to find there were no clean glasses for the bar. I had to wash the glasses by hand and dry them.

The only good thing that happened was the manager had hired two cocktail waitresses, and they would start on Friday night. I also had the weekend off!

I had worked all week and wanted to go out that Saturday night and unwind. During my lunch, I called my girlfriend, Maria, to see what she had planned to do that night and if she could get a babysitter. Maria was one of the first women I had met when I lived in the trailer park. She was bi-racial and gorgeous. She was a young mom with three bad little boys that kept her on her toes all day long. She was tired of being in the house with her kids all week and decided to go out with me. All I had to do was find a babysitter for Jazmine.

I called another friend of mine to see if she could watch Jazmine for just a few hours while I went out. Liz had a little girl the same age as mine; she usually liked to watch my daughter because it gave her child someone to play with.

When I got off that evening, I picked up Jazmine from the babysitter and went home. It was Friday; I knew my husband wasn't going to be home, either. I warmed up some dinner and bathed my daughter soon as she was done eating. I packed her a little overnight bag and took her to Liz's house. When I returned home, Marc was just about to walk out with an overnight bag of his own. He tried to tell me some lie about the guys in his department taking a friend to El Paso that weekend for a bachelor's party.

After he left, I got dressed and headed to Maria's house. She was dressed and ready to go, so we headed to the club. There was an R&B band called Roger and the Human Body performing that night; a long line had formed by the time we got there. Standing behind us were a couple of guys I had seen out before named David and his roommate Jeremy, and their dates. David and I had danced together before, and he had paid for a few drinks for me. When I first saw him, I didn't know if he were in the military because he wore his hair in cornrows that hung down past his collar. He was tall, well-built, and had a beautiful smile. I found out later that during the week, he took the braids out and wore after wetting his hair, it curled up tightly. He had flirted with me, and I with him, but that was as far as it went. But, the attraction was there.

David was with a young white woman hanging all over him, especially after she noticed I had checked him out, and we had made eye contact. The young woman that Jeremy was with I had seen around the base before and knew that she too was in the military.

When we got inside, we walked around, found a table, and sat down. David and his friends sat at a table not far from where we were sitting, and he was facing me. But I wasn't out that night to sit and make goo-goo eyes with a man. I wanted to dance, have some drinks, and enjoy myself. While on the dancefloor, I found myself dancing next to David and his girlfriend. She had watched a few episodes of Soul Train and was trying to dance like she had seen the girls on the show dance, hunching her back and snapping her hips. It was pitiful to watch. I had no choice but to put him out of his misery.

"Before tonight is over, I'm giving him my phone number," I told Maria.

"Stop it! Leave them alone!" Maria said, laughing.

When the cocktail waitress came over again, I ordered a drink to give to David. When she placed the drink in front of him and nodded towards me, he picked it up, smiled, and winked his eye. His girlfriend turned around to see who had sent the drink. Noticing it was me, she rolled her eyes, grabbed her purse, and got up angrily, walking past our table. I raised my drink and smiled.

"Go get him, girl!" Maria said.

"Come dance with me," I said, holding out my hand. He followed me to the dancefloor, and we danced.

"When you decide you want to deal with a real woman, give me a call. My name is Dedra," I said. I gave him the matchbook with my number written on the inside. I returned to my table; Maria and I left the club. After dropping her home, I headed to my place. I was exhausted and went straight to bed. Just as I got comfortable, the phone rang. I knew without even picking it up that it was David.

"Aren't you married?" he asked.

"Yes, but I am filing for a divorce and will be moving downtown the first of the month when my apartment becomes available," I replied.

"Where downtown?"

"Across from the Burger King on Otero Street."

"A duplex, dark bricks?"

"You know it?"

"I live in the first apartment; my roommate, his girl, and me."

"Wow! How convenient," I thought.

When I informed Marc I was leaving him, he chuckled. He seriously thought I would continue to stay with him and allow

35

him to disrespect me like he was doing. I had fallen out of love with him two years into this farce of a marriage. I didn't know why he thought I would continue to take it. Since he didn't take me seriously when I said I was moving out the following Thursday, he went ahead with his plans to hang out with his friends on his day off. He wasn't home when the moving van showed up at our duplex on base, packed up the house, and moved my belongings to my new apartment downtown. He wasn't going to be home until Sunday, and I would have loved to have been a fly on the wall when he walked into the empty duplex!

Maria was helping me get unpacked. By then, David and I were going pretty hot and heavy. I had met his roommates, and we had hung out together. I didn't know what happened with the little white chick he had been seeing before we starting seeing each other, but I never saw her again.

By the time David got home, Maria and I had unpacked everything, and the apartment was looking as if I had been there for a while. I was in the kitchen eating dinner – Burger King when he knocked on the door.

"You sure work fast!" he said, looking around.

Right after David and I started sleeping together, he stated he wasn't looking for a serious relationship. He was counting down his time left in the military. One year, nine months, four weeks, and six days. Sometimes, to be funny, he would throw in the minutes and the seconds he had left. We went about "kicking it" in this situationship until one night, I went to a movie with a friend of mine named Paul.

Paul and I were just friends and had no intention of being anything else. We hung out even when I was with Marc. We would go to the movies, the park, sometimes we went to El Paso to hang out and walked across the bridge into Mexico. Paul was a downlow gay guy. This was way before the "do not ask, do not tell" that came about in the Obama administration. Even though Paul acted like a heterosexual male, he was not. When the lights came on in the theatre, and we stood to leave, I saw David and his roommate, Jeremy, standing to leave. "Hey, what are you doing here?" David asked before he noticed Paul and I were together.

"Do you know Paul?" I asked.

"Yeah, I know him," he replied, turned, and walked away abruptly.

"What was that about?" Paul asked.

"I have no idea! Anyway, let's get something to eat; I'm starving!"

I didn't pay it too much mind; David was always telling me that we were just hanging out, no strings attached, so I was surprised by his jealous behavior. Paul and I went to a taco place downtown and gorged ourselves with tacos and margaritas. Afterward, he dropped me off, and I went inside. When my doorbell rang, I was just getting ready for bed. I looked out the peephole to see David standing there.

"You alone?" he asked before stepping in.

I was standing there with my men's t-shirt on and my scarf on my head, but he wanted to know if I were alone. "Of course, I'm alone!" I said, stepping to the side to let him in. "What you doing hanging out with that nigga?" "Paul and I are friends," I said, chuckling.

"I don't like you with him."

"Excuse me?" I asked, getting a bit upset. *First, he tells me that he isn't interested in a serious relationship. After he sees me with another guy, now he changes his mind?*

38

"If you are going to be seeing other guys, we may as well squash what we have."

"You're the one who said that we were just friends, hanging out," I reminded him. He got up and came to sit next to me on the sofa.

"Well, I change that now. I want to be with you and only you. But you got to want the same thing, too, or it's over."

I didn't understand men! That's how our situationship became a relationship. After that, David stopped by my apartment before he went next door to his. He spent more time at my place than his. His weekly reminders of how much time he had left had also subsided. It left me confused. Even though we were together every single day, he had never once said that he loved me.

We were spending so much time together that I began thinking I was falling in love with him. Even when I said I loved him, he would either not reply or say, "Thanks, babe!" That's not what I wanted to hear when I was professing my love for another human being.

6

EVEN THOUGH I WAS NO LONGER getting reminders of how much time he had left, it was constantly on my mind. If he wasn't interested in taking me with him when he returned to his hometown, that meant I would have to either remain in New Mexico, which I didn't want to do, or I would have to go back to New York. And if I were to go back to NY, now would be just as good a time to leave as any. Why wait for him to leave first? How pathetic would that be?

I had a lot to think about, and the only person who would listen and help me with this decision were my friends Maria, and Joyce.

"What do you think I should do?" I asked.

"Do you love him?" Maria asked.

By now, I loved him very much. I had given him my best; all of me. Yes, I loved him.

"Okay, so let me see if I understand. You love *him*. He doesn't love *you*. He doesn't want a long-term relationship. He is

40

planning on going back to his hometown when he gets out, and he hasn't asked you to come with him? What is there to think about? Take your black butt back home! You certainly don't want to continue living out here in this desert, do you? Girl, bye!" Though I agreed with her, I had a lot to think about.

I called Joyce next. "I would have never stayed as long as you have. As soon as I had left Marc's sorry behind I would have come back to be with my girl, Joyce. Remember me? Girl, stop wasting your time with these men and move on. Oh, yeah. I met a guy. He's from Ghana, Africa. He lives in London and was doing an internship at the job. We've been seeing each other. He has seven more months here. Let me tell you this, he is whupped! And I am not even going to wait around for him to ask me to go to London with him, I'm *telling* him I'm going with him. I've already put in my transfer, child!" she said laughing.

One day, David told me that he was taking a temporary tour of duty in Miami, Florida, for three weeks. He was going to need me to take him to the airport and bring his car back home.

"Don't drive it or anything, just bring it back and park it," he said, making that clear. I had a car; I didn't need to drive his car, anyway. The first week he was gone, he called me every night and morning. During the next two weeks, the calls were less frequent. It was four days between the time of our last call and the one he made to tell me what time he wanted me to pick him up from the airport.

On his first night back, he seemed preoccupied. I figured he was tired and just didn't think anything of it. When the telephone rang a few days after he had been home, I was at his house talking to his roommate's girlfriend, Diane. She was in the bathroom and yelled for me to get it. I answered the phone, and a woman asked if David was home. I told her he hadn't gotten home from work yet.

"Is this Diane?" she asked.

"No, it's not. Would you like to leave her a message also," I asked?

"No. I just remembered some of the names of David's friends when he was here in Miami. I thought that was who you are."

"Give me your name, and I will tell him you called." I reached for a piece of paper and a pen.

"This is Janine. I'm his girlfriend." I was surprised by that confession.

"Okay. I can assume he has your phone number?"

"Who are you again?"

"I *used* to be his girlfriend," I said and hung up.

That night when David came by the apartment to eat dinner, I casually told him Janine had called. I could see him turn six shades of red while he scanned my face, looking for my reaction. I placed two pieces of fried chicken on his plate and asked if he wanted a salad.

"No, I'll just have some string beans and rice." I continued fixing his plate and then fixed my baby's plate. I cut her chicken off the bone and put her plate on the high chair. I fixed my plate, casually sat down, and acted all nonchalant.

"That's a girl I met that worked at the NCO club down in Miami."

I bit my chicken, all the while watching him and how he was squirming.

"She was nice to me and the fellows," he continued. I smiled and nodded.

"I think she said her ex-husband had been in the military or something like that," he went on.

I just sat there, slowing chewing my food and enjoying this. All the while, thinking it was time to head back to New York before he left. I made a mental note to contact my ex-husband the next day to get that lined up. I would also need him to put my furniture in storage and sell my car. All the while, I was planning my departure. David continued talking about how helpful Janine had been to him and his friends.

Later, as we lay in bed beside each other, I told him that I had a headache. I turned to face the wall and went peacefully to sleep. When he left for work, I called my ex-husband and told him to get me a plane ticket; I was ready to go back home now. That was two months, one week and four days before David's time at Holloman Air Force Base was to end.

I never said one word to him about my plans until three days after I had my plane ticket in my hand and the schedule for my apartment to be packed up and stored.

I waited until we were getting ready for bed one night. I was in the bathroom, brushing my teeth, and he was stepping out of the shower.

"Oh yeah, I'm going to need a ride to the airport on Saturday morning. I have a flight at noon," I said and rinsed out my mouth.

As I stood up, he was standing there, drying off and looking confused.

"Where are you going?" he asked.

"I decided to go back home." I wiped my mouth and went to my bedroom with him right behind me.

"And you are just now telling me?"

"I wanted to make sure everything was in order." I threw back the covers and got in the bed. He stood there, continuing to dry himself off, and then pulled on his sweatpants and a T-shirt.

"I'm sleeping at home tonight," he said. I followed him to the door and locked it. I went back to bed. My phone ringing at twothirty that morning woke me up.

"Hello?" I asked sleepily.

"Hey, are you awake? Let me in," David said. I stumbled to the door, unlocked it, and went back to bed. When he got inside, he stripped out of his clothes and curled up against my body, pulling me into his arms.

"I love you," he whispered just before I fell back to sleep.

Now I was confused and ticked off! We had been together for over a year, and not once in all of that time had he ever said he loved me. I lay awake most of the night, letting the tears roll down my face.

The day I was leaving, he took off from work to drive me to the airport in El Paso. He carried my daughter in his arms and held my hand tightly as we made our way to our gate. We talked as we waited for my flight to board.

"When I get back home and get on my feet, I want to send for you. I think we can make this work," he said. I looked at him as he spoke, but that phone call, that Janine chick was fresh in my mind. I knew I wasn't anything special if he could have gone to Florida for just a few weeks and get with another woman just like that. No, he might send for me, but I certainly wasn't going anywhere to be with him.

I had been married to a man who I took care of like he was a king, and he treated me like I was a servant. He couldn't walk past another woman without making eye contact with her, smiling at her right in front of me as if I were no one special. No, the next man I got with was going to be different. If he didn't treat me like I was someone special, I wasn't going to give him the time of day.

My days of catering to men were over.

When the flight attendant announced our flight was boarding, David held me tightly and kissed me. I saw tears in his eyes, but it was too much, too little, too late.

I got on that flight and never once thought about going to be with him when he returned to his hometown. That wasn't the way it was going to turn out. I was hurt, and I couldn't hide it. I didn't want to hide it. In the four years I had lived in New Mexico, many people had hurt me. It wasn't just these two men who had hurt me. I had allowed myself to get caught up in all kinds of foolishness, and I had no one to blame but myself.

By the time the plane landed at LaGuardia, I looked forward to seeing a familiar face, but it wasn't my cousin who picked me up from the airport. Standing there, waiting for me, was an old boyfriend from back in the day, also named Marc. I could feel myself sinking, and there was no solidness underneath my feet. He helped me with my luggage and hailed a taxi.

"Where is Roger?" I asked. I knew he must have contacted him to be the one here to get us.

"He had something to do and asked me to come to get you.
That's okay, isn't it?" he asked.
"Sure."

He held out his arms awkwardly.

"Okay, you want to hug me!" I said, chuckling.

We hugged, and I pulled away as I heard him inhale as if sniffing me. *Dude!* He held the door for me, and we got into the taxi.

Upon arrival at my aunt's house, my daughter was sleeping. He carried her upstairs. I got the two pieces of luggage out of the back of the taxi.

Aunt Gladys met us at the door, smiling, happy to see me. I hated being back in New York, but I had nowhere else to go. I certainly didn't want to go to Texas and stay with my mother. My dad lived in a one-bedroom apartment, so he didn't' have any room for us. Nor did I want to go to South Carolina and stay with my grandmother. So, here I was in familiar territory and hoping all would be well this time.

After getting settled in my old bedroom, I just wanted to get some real Chinese food in my mouth, take a sleeping pill, and sleep for the next ten hours. However, my Aunt Gladys and cousins all seemed to have other plans. As they got off work, they began showing up, each bringing a bottle of liquor. I set up a bar for them with ice, glasses, slices of lemon and oranges, and fixed drinks for everyone. We ate Chinese and Jamaican foods and talked about old times.

Marc and I went way back. However, he had done me just like every man in my life had done. He was my first serious boyfriend. I was faithful to him, and he, not so much. Therefore, I was certainly not interested in going down that road with him again. Finally, around two that morning, after having had only one drink, I excused myself and went to bed. My daughter was sprawled out across the bed, snoring softly. I eased her over toward the back of the bed and got in and went fast to sleep. It was then I realized I hadn't even called David to let him know I had arrived safely. Oops!

When I woke up the next morning, my head was killing me. It had been a while since I had drunk straight vodka and then went to bed. I went to the kitchen to get a glass of water. From the living room, someone said, "Good morning." Marc had spent the night on the couch.

"Did you get wasted?" I asked, standing behind the door because I wasn't fully dressed.

"Just a little," he said. I remembered how wasted he used to get back in the day. No, he wasn't just a little wasted. He probably was pissy drunk before he stopped drinking. That was another reason I didn't want him. I chuckled and went back to my bedroom, where I got back into the bed and fell to sleep again.

7

"IT'S BEEN A WEEK. WHEN are you going to start looking for a job? You can't just lay around crying all day and sleeping," my aunt said that morning before going to work.

I was depressed! Work was the farthest thing from my mind. This was the third time she had said I needed to get a job! Hadn't she had a broken heart before? Dang! Leave me alone about a job already, will ya? I wanted to scream!

She would take something out to cook. At first, I would just put it in the fridge and let her cook it when she got home. I just really didn't want to be bothered with anyone. I was drained, mentally, and physically. I was tired!

I called my daddy; I thought he would understand how I felt.

"Have you found a job yet?" he asked. I knew Aunt Gladys had probably said something to him about me just lying around crying, and feeling sorry for myself.

"No, I haven't looked for one. I'm depressed!" I replied.

"You might feel better if you were working?" Oh, God! He sounded just like my aunt. I knew she was only thinking of the extra money she would get from me if I were working.

Finally, I got tired of it and decided I needed to get away for a weekend. I just needed to be around folks who knew me, loved me, and wasn't going to be asking me about no freaking job!

I called my friends from New Mexico, who had moved to Hampton right before I had left, Wayne and Sherita. I missed Wayne. When I needed to really get a man's opinion on something going on in my life, I always called Wayne. "Sure, come on down!" Sherita said.

"Are you sure?" I asked.

"Yeah, it will be fun. My girl, Denise, and her boyfriend Mike from Queens is also down here visiting. We can hang out tonight and have some fun."

After I hung up with her, I called People's Express Airlines to see what flights they had that day going to Virginia and what time the flight was leaving. They had a flight leaving in exactly three hours. That left me enough time to put some clothes in a suitcase, take my daughter to my father's house, and get to the airport. I called Daddy to see if he was home. Then I walked down to his apartment.

When we got there, he was sitting in the backyard in a rickety old chair. I said I needed to get away for the weekend and asked if he could watch Jazmine.

"Sure. Call me when you get there and don't take no wooden nickels," he said. I left my daughter, and her clothes, and nearly ran back to my aunt's. I got my suitcase and took a taxi to the airport.

In an hour, I was landing in Norfolk, Virginia. "Sherita and her friend, Denise, were at the airport to pick me up. We hugged each other and she introduced me to her friend. Denise and I also hugged each other. On the way back to her place, we stopped at a fish market, and she got fish to fry for dinner. I had eaten Sherita's cooking before, and she wasn't that great of a cook. She made the spaghetti and a salad; I fried fish, made the coleslaw, and some hush puppies. While we were in the kitchen cooking and cutting up, a friend of Wayne's came over named Kevin. I saw him from the kitchen but didn't meet him until the dinner was done and the table set. I could see that Wayne was trying to match us up, or at least get us to sit next to each other at the dinner table.

Kevin was tall, medium built, and brown-skinned. As the platters of food got passed around the table, everyone was talking, and usually over each other. They complimented my food and that made me feel very good.

After we had cleaned the kitchen, Sherita asked the guys to take us out. There was a baseball game on that night, and they didn't want to go anywhere. Wayne told Kevin to take us out since he wasn't interested in the game. I hadn't packed any going out clubbing clothes, so we decided to just go to the NCO club on the base. All I had was dark blue jeans, a white pair of jeans and a skirt to wear on the flight. I decided to wear the white jeans. I freshened my makeup, put on hoop earrings, and slipped on some heels. I checked myself in the mirror, and I figured for a Friday night on a military base, I looked okay. We all wore jeans and white t-shirts to the club.

Once we got outside, Sherita decided she wanted to sit in the front with Kevin, but he held the door for me and blocked her with his arm. She relented and got in the backseat behind him. As we were driving to the base, she began flirting with Kevin.

She wasn't in her seatbelt; she kept touching his neck and trying to kiss him.

"C'mon, girl! What's wrong with you? I'm going to tell Wayne on you," he kept saying and pushing her hands away. She was trying to rub his chest and just being a nuisance.

"Let's stop to a liquor store and get a bottle of rum before we get to the club," she suggested.

"I don't think you need any more rum; you're already acting like a fool," Kevin said. We stopped anyway; Denise and I got out with her, leaving Kevin inside of the car.

"Girl, what's up with you? You know that's your man's boy? Why are you acting like that?" Denise asked Sherita.

"I'm just trying to see how far he will let me go," she responded.

"Well, he doesn't like it, and you're looking stupid!" Denise said. I figured that would be all that was needed to get her to leave the man alone. But while he was driving the car, she continued pulling on him and trying to kiss him. It didn't seem to matter to her that he was telling her to leave him alone and to stop it; he was going to tell Wayne.

Once we got to the NCO club, there was a crowd of people already there. The DJ was playing all the latest hits, but no one was dancing. As Prince's song, "Controversy," came on, I grabbed Sherita's hand to dance. I had no idea it went against the military rules that women could not dance together on a base. We were kindly escorted out of the club by two bouncers.

"I'm taking you ladies home, I have had enough," Kevin said. He joined us outside, where we were trying to explain to the bouncers that we were not gay. We just wanted to get the party started!

It was only midnight, way too early to turn in, so Sherita told Kevin to take us to get something to eat, and then we could hang out at his place.

"I'll take y'all to get something to eat, but I don't know about that last part. You don't know how to act," he told Sherita.

We stopped at a fast-food restaurant and ordered burgers and fries. We ended up going to Kevin's barracks anyway. His room was on the third floor, and there was no elevator. Sherita was talking loudly and trying to get ahead of me so she could continue her relentless flirting with Kevin. He kept pushing her away and telling her to stop it. I was embarrassed for her, but she seemed oblivious to his reactions.

In Kevin's room, there were two full-size beds, a dresser, two chairs, and a desk. There was a nightstand that separated the beds, and his windows were opened, and the curtains pulled back. There was also a half bath in his room. Showers were down the hallway. As we made our way to his room, some of his fellow soldiers began teasing him about having three women with him.

"It's not like that; trust me!" he replied.

When we got inside of his room, I asked if I could sit on his bed.

"Yeah, sure. Make yourself at home. I removed my shoes, sat back, leaned my back against the wall, and opened my bag of food. He sat beside me, and Denise sat on the bed across from us. Sherita came and jumped on the bed beside him and put her arms around his neck.

"Will you please stop it! Damn! What is wrong with you?" he asked.

I could tell he was finally getting frustrated with her.

"I'm not going to tell Wayne if you don't!" she said and leaned inward, trying to kiss him.

"Stop it!" he said, this time with a bit of anger in his voice.

"Are you gay?"

"No, I'm not gay. You're my best friend's wife! Stop it, or I will take your black behind back home! I mean it! That's enough!" he said angrily. She got up and went to sit beside Denise. Her face was red with embarrassment. "Finally," I thought. She was getting on my nerves!

"Where are you visiting from again? I forgot!" he asked.

"New York," I said between bites of my burger.

"Did you all know each other in New York?" he asked, referring to Wayne, Sherita, and me.

"No, we met at Holloman Air Force Base in New Mexico," I answered. He smiled.

"I was stationed there too. What year were you there?"

"I was there from 1983 to 1987. I wasn't in the military, my ex-husband was."

"I missed you somehow."

"Sherita, do you have any ketchup?" I asked. She threw me two packs of ketchup. "Are you okay?" Now she seemed to be angry with me.

"You asked for ketchup, and I gave it to you," she snapped.

There was no need for her to get upset with me! I was a single woman, and she was not. She was also the wife of his best friend. Surely, she had sense enough to know that whatever she had in mind was not going to happen.

"What do you do in New York?" Kevin asked.

"You really want to know?" I asked.

"Yeah."

"I cry a lot. I go to bed crying and wake up crying. I also have a little girl whose two-and-a-half. I just got back there about a month ago. I'll be okay. You know how it is sometimes."

Dang! After I said it, I thought about how pathetic it sounded. *I go to bed crying and wake up crying!* Denise and Sherita were talking softly on the other side of the room, but I couldn't make out what they were saying. I hoped they hadn't heard me.

"Those fries smell good. Can I get one?" Kevin asked me.

"No, you can't have none of my fries! You were right there and could have gotten some!" I teased him. He reached toward my bag, trying to get some of my fries.

I took the bag and put it under my blouse!

"Now, try to get them!" I said, laughing.

He was trying to get the fries from me. I was laughing and holding my shirt down, not that he was trying to go up under it. But when I came up for air, I looked across the room at Sherita. Instead of her smiling about it, she was glaring at me. I felt uncomfortable by her stare but wasn't sure why she was looking at me like that. Before I could say anything else, she slid off the bed and told Denise to walk her outside; they were going to sit in the car.

"What's wrong with her?" I asked Kevin. He got up from the bed and locked the door behind them. I took the fries from under my blouse and held them out to Kevin.

"You still want a fry?" I asked, laughing. He took the fries and put about six in his mouth at once. "Hey! You ate all my fries!" I said and pretended to start crying.

He caught me off guard when he pulled me into his arms and hugged me. He was just holding me. His face was against my face. After several seconds, I pulled away.

"Thanks," I whispered.

8

KEVIN KISSED ME. FIRST ON the cheek, then close to my lips. I wasn't expecting him to kiss me. Was he drunk? I couldn't remember if he drunk any of the rum. I didn't see him do so. I didn't taste any on him.

I melted into Kevin, and he filled every pore in my body with something I had never felt before. We didn't say anything as he removed my clothing and kissed every part of me.

Two hours later, I lay there totally drained and wet.

"I'm going to take them home. I'll be right back. Don't answer the door if anyone knocks, okay?"

He went to the bathroom and came out dressed in sweatpants and a hoodie. He closed and locked the door. I waited a few minutes to make sure he wasn't coming back, and then I got up. My clothes were scattered all over the floor. I picked them up and laid them on the other bed neatly.

What just happened? Did I just have sex with this man? I went to the bathroom and turned on the hot water. I looked at my reflection in the mirror and noticed he had left marks on my neck in several places. I splashed the water on my face and wondered where he kept his washcloths. Being nosy, I opened the medicine cabinet. He had a bottle of Tylenol. Several bottles of vitamins, shaving cream, and razor blades. He had some Band-Aids. A box of condoms! I ran back to the bed to look for used condoms. Did he use a condom? Two wrappers were laying on the nightstand. I was relieved knowing that at least. I looked in his dresser and found some towels and washcloths. I got a cloth and went back to the bathroom. I washed up well and got dressed.

I was sitting on the other bed, watching TV when he returned. It was close to 3:30 in the morning.

"How come you switched beds?" he asked, smiling. That bed was soaking wet. I had thrown back the covers to allow it to dry. He took off his sneakers. While he was bent over doing that, I sat there as my foot swung back and forth nervously. He took his socks off, rolled them up, put them neatly inside his shoes, and put them in the closet. He seemed so disciplined.

"Do you want to take a shower?" he asked. I knew the showers were down the hallway, and all the people in the building were men. Noticing my hesitation, he assured me that he would protect me.

He handed me a towel, and I followed him down the quiet hallway to the shower area. He turned on the light and stood against the door, watching me. I just stood there.

"Go on!" he said.

Okay, he was going to watch.

I stepped out of my jeans, and the rest of my clothing and turned on the shower. There were tiny bars of different kinds of soap like ones you would find at a hotel on a shelf. He removed the wrapper and handed me one. I began lathering up as he stood there, smiling and watching me. Since he wanted to watch, I did a little dance and shimmy for him. He was smiling broadly now.

"You should have told me the shower came with a dance, I would have gotten me some one's!" he said, laughing.

I rinsed off and wrapped a towel around me. After I got out, he stepped into the shower.

"You can go back to the room. Lock the door, okay?"

I made my way safely to the room and locked the door. When he returned to the room, I was still wrapped in the towel, and he was wrapped in a towel as well.

He laid a fresh towel on the wet bed and said he would sleep over there. But he came to sit beside me.

"You look nervous like you're about ready to jump out of the window or something," he said, smiling.

"I'm cool," I said.

"You sure?"

"Yes, I'm fine. It's a bit chilly in here."

Kevin looked in his drawer and gave me a big red T-shirt to put on. He turned off the TV and turned on the radio to an R&B station that was still playing love songs. He turned the light on in the bathroom and pulled the door shut halfway. Kevin turned off the overhead light; now, we were in a nearly dark room. He reached for me again, and I melted into him once again.

This time, I tried to remember every single second of what was going on. Everything about him was different. It was catching me in my chest, like the feeling a kid gets on Christmas day as she opens a package, and it's her favorite doll. The one she's been asking for all year! I couldn't hold him tight enough or close enough. And I cried and laughed all at once.

We lay there afterward; he was raised on one elbow, looking at me. Neither of us saying anything. He was just looking at me, and I was just looking at him. He pulled me into his arms and fell asleep peacefully. Just before I dozed off I realized I had known him less than a day and I had given him my whole cookie!

When I woke up, Kevin was sitting on the other bed, watching me. "Hey, sleepyhead," he said. "I don't know about you, but I am starving. Get dressed so we can get some breakfast." I freshened up in his bathroom and got dressed

He held my hand as we walked to his car, heading out to get breakfast. It was nearly one in the afternoon. As we walked into the diner, I slid into the booth, and he slid in beside me. He picked up the menu and opened it, humming a song I didn't recognize.

"I think I can eat four eggs and a steak!" he said, chuckling.

"I think I can, too!" I said. He kissed me gently on the lips. We were interrupted by the waitress coming to take our order.

After breakfast, we drove to the beach and walked along the shore, holding hands. We sat down in an area where no one was nearby.

"What would you like to do tomorrow?" he asked.

"I'm leaving tomorrow," I replied.

"Why? Aren't you having a good time?"

"I only came for the weekend. My flight leaves tomorrow afternoon around one if I'm not mistaken. I have to check my ticket."

"Can't you stay a little longer? We are just getting to know one another. I can see about getting next week off. I would like to get to know you better. Please," he said, pouting like a little kid.

"Okay, I'll call my dad and ask if he can watch my daughter until next Sunday." He pulled me into his arms and held me tightly.

When we got back to his barracks, I called my dad to see if he could watch Jazmine until next Sunday.

"Yeah, we're having a good time. We've picked some fresh tomatoes, and she helped me make a salad. Well, she made more of a mess than she made of the salad. But sure, stay and have some fun. Love you, babe," he said.

Kevin got us a hotel room near the beach. After checking into the room, he dropped me off at Sherita's so I could get my bag.

"I'll be back in an hour," he said before driving off. Sherita was sitting on the porch, smoking a cigarette.

"Hey, ladybug!" I said as I approached her. She tapped the cigarette, letting the ashes fall to the ground. She blew the smoke in my direction. I coughed and fanned it away.

"Look what the dog drug home," she said.

"What did I tell you about them cancer sticks?" I teased, ignoring her rude comment.

"And what did I tell you about whoring?"

"I wasn't whoring for your information. Where is Denise and ..."

"They went back to Queens this morning. Ain't you too old to have a neck full of hickies?"

"I just came to get my bag. I'm going to stay with Kevin. We got a room on the beach."

"Whatever! It's by the door," she said, motioning with her head towards the door.

Sure enough, she had placed my bag by the door. I went inside to get it and returned to the porch. I sat on the step instead of sitting up on the porch with her. She was hurling one insult after another at me. I was trying hard not to get angry with her, but she was pushing it.

She dished out her final insult and went into her house, closing and locking the door behind her! I could not believe she had gotten this upset with me because I had spent time with Kevin. I didn't have the energy to go back and forth with her. I got enough of that negative energy back in Brooklyn. When Kevin came to get me, I was still sitting on the porch.

"Sherita is ticked off!" I said, getting into the car.

"She'll be okay. She's just tripping," he said.

"Was that the first time she had ever tried to make a pass with you?"

"The very first. I was just as surprised as you. I'm not even going to tell Wayne how she acted. It was what it was. Don't

say anything to him, either. They are having enough problems."
I hadn't planned to tell Wayne how Sherita was acting anyway.

Seeing the way Sherita had approached Kevin, had me wondering if she was trying to make me jealous or hoping to make her husband jealous. Whatever the case was, it didn't work on Kevin. I doubted her approach would work on anyone.

9

AFTER KEVIN AND I HAD CHECKED into the Marriott Hotel in Virginia Beach, we went up to our room on the fourth floor. We had a view of the ocean, and it was beautiful. I could hardly wait to let the water run across my feet. I changed into sandals, and we went down to walk along the beach and talk. Kevin carried a blanket he had taken from his room.

We spread it out and sat down to talk and sip the bottle of Reunite I had put in my purse.

"Are your parents still alive?" I asked.

"My mother is, but my dad isn't. He died two years ago. He died young," he said, looking out at the water.

"What happened to him?"

"He worked himself to death. When he was a kid growing up in Georgia, he and his siblings had to work to help out their parents. They worked in the fields. He swore it would be different when he had kids. He told me he and his brother and sister never got a chance to play and just be kids. They had to work and help pay bills, buy their clothes, and stuff like that. So, when he had us, everything we wanted to do, he made it happen. He worked overtime all the time. Sometimes he would be gone when we got up for school, and we would be in bed by the time he got home from work. But I was able to play every sport my school offered from the first grade to high school. He died a week after my youngest sister, Traci, graduated from high school. It was like he waited for all six of us to get out of school, and then his body quit on him. He was tired," he said, his voice trailing off.

I moved closer to him and put my arms around him. He patted my hand and turned his face away, but I could tell it still bothered him.

"Have you ever been married?" I asked.

"Me? Naw! I haven't met anyone I wanted to spend my life with, until now," he said.

"I have wine! You want some wine?" I asked, changing the subject.

"Hey, I'm trying to get my Mack on, and you're telling me about some wine!" he said, laughing. I put the bottle back in the bag.

"Mack on, brother!" I teased.

I was falling in love with this man! This man was falling in love with me! Never, ever had I felt this way about anyone. I loved the way he looked at me and the way I felt safe with him. I loved his loving. I knew if he asked me to, I would come back to Hampton in a heartbeat!

For the next six days, we loved on one another again and again and again. We talked and got to know one another. He had shared so much with me about his family; I felt as if I knew them personally. I shared with him how I didn't know my mother because she was gone by the time I was two-years-old. All I knew about her was horrible things told to me by family on my father's side. He had never said anything bad about her, but the rest of them certainly had. When we were not talking, we were loving on each other.

The week went by quickly. The night before my flight, we went shopping for a dress and shoes so he could take me to a nice restaurant for dinner. "I sure am going to miss him," I thought as he told funny stories and smiled broadly at watching me cracking up.

Back at the hotel, he turned to his favorite radio station; we danced slowly, holding each other tightly. The fresh smell of the ocean was intoxicating. I hated this was our last night together. However, I truly enjoyed every single minute of being in his arms.

After breakfast, we went to the airport, riding there in silence. It had been an incredible time, one I didn't want to end, but I had to go back home. I had an eighteen-month-old daughter depending on me. I needed to get it together. Since Kevin hadn't asked me to come back to Hampton, I was willing to make the trips down to visit him. But, right now, I had to get back home. All of these thoughts were going through my head. Should I ask him if I could come back and be with him? I thought about the job market. I thought about a place to live. I didn't want to make the first move, but I loved him enough to do that. I said a silent prayer to God that if this man loved me, let him ask me to come back.

When we arrived at the airport, I had to stop at the ticket counter to get my ticket reissued. There was a $25 fee, and he paid it. Holding my hand, we walked to my gate area and took a seat away from the other travelers.

"Wow! This is it. I just want you to know I had a great "weekend," and I hope, no, I want you to come and live here in Hampton. I can get you and your daughter an apartment, and we can continue to get to know one another. But I don't want this to be the end of this time we had together. I got you something." He handed me a bright pink envelope.

"Don't open it until you get home, okay. I love you," he said and kissed me tenderly.

"I love you, too. And yes, I will come back. I don't want this to end either."

"Flight 127 is now boarding. Passengers, please report to Gate 12 now. Flight 127 is now boarding!"

I remembered I didn't have his phone number. I looked in my bag for a pen but didn't have one.

"Just give it to me; I can remember it," I said.

"C'mon? Let me find a pen." He went up to the agent, but she didn't have a pen.

"Kevin, I can remember it; just give it to me," I assured him. That had been my thing. I could remember numbers without writing them down.

"Okay, you better remember it! 757-621-1341. You got it?"

"Yes! 757-621-1341, see? I love you, babe."

He held me again for one last kiss.

"Come on, guys; I have to close the door," the agent said. On the plane, I tried to see if I could see Kevin from the window, but I didn't see him. I was missing him already.

10

THE PLANE ARRIVED AT LAGUARDIA, and I hurried to a taxi and went straight to Daddy's house. I had missed my daughter, and this was truly the longest I had ever been gone from her. When I got to my Daddy's place, he buzzed me up. He was sitting on the sofa with my daughter's head in his lap, and there was a cloth on her forehead.

"She woke up during the night crying, and I noticed she had a fever. This morning, I got some baby Tylenol from the drugstore and ginger ale. She's been sleeping off and on throughout the day," he said.

I picked her up, gave her a big kiss, and noticed she was hot.

"Thanks for watching her for me. I'm going to take her to the ER and make sure she's okay. I'll call you later, Daddy. Love you, and thanks a bunch for watching her for me."

"Call me and let me know she's okay."

When I got to my Aunt Gladys' house, she was finishing cooking her Sunday dinner.

"You finally remembered where you lived?" she asked sarcastically. I wasn't in the mood for her mess.

"Jazmine has a fever. I'm going to freshen her up and take her to the ER," I said, ignoring her comments.

She wiped her hands on the towel she was holding and touched Jasmine's back and legs.

"She's burning up! But you know what? I bet it's just an ear infection. My boys used to get them all the time. I didn't even bother to take them to the ER. I gave them some baby aspirin and put a warm compress on their ear," she said.

"Well, I'm taking her to the ER." I laid her down on my bed and removed her sweaty clothes. I went to the bathroom with a washcloth and soaped it up. When I went back to the bedroom, Aunt Know It All was trying to make Jazmine smile.

"See, ain't nothing wrong with her. Just get some baby aspirin," she said.

"We don't give babies aspirin when they have a fever now. I'm taking her to the ER!" I said.

"Well, let me finish my dinner, and I'll take you."

In the meantime, I got the phone from the kitchen wall and walked back to my bedroom with it.

"You better not be making no long-distance call!" she yelled.

I wasn't thinking about anything she said. I was going to call Kevin and let him know I got home safe.

I dialed 757 and could not, for the life of me, remember the rest of the numbers. I pressed the button to end the call and think.

"Did you hear what I said? You better not be making no long distance calls on my phone! You ain't got no job and ain't even looking for one!" she yelled again.

757-6 … 757-4! I couldn't remember, and she wouldn't shut up. I took the phone back to the kitchen and hung it up noisily.

"Are you trying to break the phone?" she shouted.

By the time I finished washing Jazmine up and getting her dressed, Aunt Gladys was standing in the doorway with her handbag and keys.

On the way to the emergency room, she was telling me how it was just an ear infection. All I had to do was put some warm compresses on her ear, and she would be just fine.

After we got to ghetto Saint Mary's Hospital, I knew we would be there for a while. I signed us in and waited away from most of the sick folk. My aunt struck up a conversation with a woman her age, who was waiting for her daughter to pick her up.

"This is my niece and my great-niece. She came home from gallivanting around the world, and the baby had a touch of fever. I told her that it's probably just an ear infection. You know these little ones get them ear infections. I have five sons, and not once in all of their lives have I ever taken them to the ER because they had a fever. But you can't tell these young people anything today. They already know everything," she said. As soon as the woman acted like she was going to reply, Aunt Gladys cut her off to repeat the same thing.

To our surprise, we were called within a few minutes of being there.

"You can wait here," I said. I just didn't want to hear her go on and on and not let me speak for myself. But she got up and came with us. While the nurse was taking Jazmine's vitals, Aunt Gladys was telling her it was just an ear infection.

Fifteen minutes later, an Asian doctor pulled back the curtain and entered. I started explaining to him that my baby had a fever, but Aunt Gladys cut me off.

"She has an ear infection. She walks around most of the day, sucking on a bottle. That's all it is, just an ear infection," she said. Without even touching my child, he took out his prescription pad and wrote down a prescription for Amoxicillin.

"You're not going to examine her?" I asked.

"Your mom has examined her. We have patients that have much more serious problems. You all have a nice evening," he said and walked out.

"See, I told you!" Aunt Gladys said.

We went to the hospital's pharmacy and got the prescription filled and went home. I gave my daughter the medicine. Within an hour, she was throwing up.

"Mix it in apple sauce or something. And put a warm compress on her little ears," Auntie said, coming into my bedroom without knocking on the door.

I couldn't take it! I turned off the light and tried to get my daughter to go to sleep. Once the house was quiet, I tiptoed into the kitchen and sat at the table with the phone in my hand.

I dialed 757-62 ... I just could not remember the number. I dialed 4-1-1 and asked directory assistance if they had a number for Kevin Brown in Hampton, Virginia. The operator told me that his number was private.

"This is an emergency."

"I'm sorry, ma'am. His number is private!"

I put the phone back on the receiver and went to bed crying. I regretted not writing down his number!

The next day, her fever had gone up to 103 degrees. I decided to take her back to the ER. Aunt Gladys drove us again. All the way there she ran her mouth. I wished she would shut up! She hadn't been to medical school, and just because she had five sons didn't make her an expert about medical care, either.

This time, we went to Killer Kings County.

"This time, can you be quiet and let the doctors diagnose my child. That doctor didn't even touch Jazmine," I said.

"He didn't have to examine her to know that when a baby has a fever, and they still on the bottle, they more than likely have an ear infection," she said.

And once again, she told the lazy doctor what was wrong with Jazmine. He turned to me and said, "Listen to your mom. Give the antibiotic a chance to work, and she will be fine in about two or three days."

I wanted to scream!

On Tuesday, I saw that Jazmine was still feverish; I called my cousin, Rob, to see if he could take me to Fort Hamilton's Military Hospital. While Aunt Gladys was at work, that is where we went.

The doctor, who came in to take care of her, was thorough. Dr. Nugyen ran all kinds of tests. He even did a spinal tap to rule out meningitis. After the test results came back, he looked relieved, but then he became solemn.

"I have good news and some not so good. First, the good news. She doesn't have an ear infection nor meningitis. However, I consulted with a pediatrician and with the high fever, and look here," he said, holding up Jazmine's hand and showing me the white lines in her fingernails.

"The high fever, the lines in her fingernails leads us to one conclusion. The baby has Kawasaki's disease."

I had never heard of that before, and the name itself frightened me.

"There are two military hospitals that have successfully treated Kawasaki's disease. One is in Washington, DC, and the other is at Fort Sam Houston Army Base in San Antonio, Texas. We've spoken with the Red Cross, and they will pay for your airline travel, and also pay for you to stay at Billeting."

My mother lived in Texas. I hadn't seen her in twenty years, but at least if I were in Texas, I would be able to see her. I wasn't even thinking how close DC was to Virginia. I just didn't think about it. I chose the hospital in Texas. Before I left the hospital, I got some quarters and went to a payphone to try Kevin's number again. I still couldn't remember it. So, I called Sherita.

"Hey, girl. I only have a couple of quarters. Can you take down this number and call me back?" I gave her the number to the payphone and hung up. A woman walking by told me that these phones are not set up that way.

"She won't be able to call you back," she said and walked on.

After I got back to Aunt Gladys' house, I sneaked and called Sherita again.

"Can you do me a favor? Call Kevin and tell him to give me a call at this number. I'm leaving tonight to go to Texas because Jazmine is sick, and the hospital they are sending us to is in San Antonio, Texas. He has to call me right now because I have to pack and get out of here."

"What's wrong with the baby?"

"She was diagnosed with something called Kawasaki's disease. I have to go, okay. Thanks, Sherita." I hurried and threw our clothes in the suitcase and hoped that Kevin would call in the next few minutes. But he didn't. In an hour, my cousin came to take us to the airport, I felt like I had just missed Kevin's call.

On the way to San Antonio, Jazmine was sick on the plane. She kept throwing up and crying. We were moved to the back of the plane, so we didn't disturb the other passengers. I was worried about her.

When we walked into the terminal, there was a young African American man from the Red Cross waiting for us, holding a sign with my name on it. He drove us to the hospital.

After getting my daughter signed in, we were led to the Pediatric ICU. I changed her into a hospital gown. A nurse came in and took her vital signs. It took two nurses to insert the IV into her hand. I stood in the hallway and cried for my baby. When her cries became whimpers, I entered the room again, just in time to see her snatch the IV out of her hand.

The nurses worked to get it inserted again, and her free hand was placed in restraint to the side rail. Jazmine had worn herself out and just lay there looking tired. Once she finally saw me there, she tried to get up and reach for me. While the nurses continued working on her and making her comfortable, I went around to the other side of the bed and soothed her.

Jazmine finally went to sleep, so I went to the nurses' station to see if I could leave for a few minutes to get something to eat, or if I should wait for the doctor to come by.

"The doctor will not be around until about six this evening, so you have plenty of time to get something to eat. You look tired. Why don't you get a couple of hours of rest? She's going to be sleeping for a while. Go on! Everything will be okay," she assured me.

While I waited for the elevator, I thought about how my life had changed. Two days ago, I was having a wonderful time with a man I had fallen in love with. And today, I'm in another state, in the ICU with my daughter, fighting for her life. Nurses were rushing down the hallways. I could hear the cries of children in pain. I could hear their parents crying. A doctor darted down the hallway to a room. The voice on the intercom announced some type of code, and several nurses rushed into action. I had to look away. When the elevator finally arrived, I stepped inside quickly and let the doors close. I leaned against the wall and fought back the tears.

Outside, the air was hot and humid. I rushed to the Mess Hall, which was the only place I could use my ID to eat. It was a little after breakfast; the crowd had died down. I got in line and picked up a tray and my silverware. I was about to get a bowl of oatmeal when I remembered I hadn't eaten since yesterday. I was starving and needed to eat. I got a burger, fries, and a slice of pineapple cake. I looked around for a table way off by the window where no one else was sitting. I sat down and began eating.

I wrapped my cake in a napkin and walked back to my room because I wanted to call Sherita and give her the phone number to give to Kevin.

"Sherita, hey. How are you doing? Can you give this number to Kevin, please?" I read her the number.
"Had he called you before you left New York?" she asked.

"No."

"Doesn't that tell you something? But I will give him this number too. How's my baby doing?"

"What is that supposed to mean?"

"You're acting like you are in love with this dude! It's kind of pathetic. But I will give him the number."

I hung up the phone, angry that she would say something like that to me. Even for Sherita, it was mean. I wanted to curse her out!

I took a nap, and when I woke up, I had slept for four hours. I splashed water on my face, brushed my teeth, and walked back to the hospital. A nurse told me there were books in the room two doors past the bathrooms if I wanted to read to Jazmine. There were also toys, but she wasn't in the mood to play with any of them. I sat beside her bed and read her favorite book, *Good Night Moon*. Each time I finished, she would say, "Again," and I would read it again until she was finally sleeping. I laid the recliner back and fell asleep, also. By the time I woke up, it was after midnight. The doctor had made his rounds, and I had missed him. The nurse told me what he had determined.

"She is still in critical condition, but her vital signs are stable right now. We are going to be keeping an eye on her and making sure that they don't go up. As long as they don't go up ... We have her sedated right now because she was restless and trying to get the IV out. If you want to, why don't you go back to the room and get some rest in a real bed? We will call if there is any change."

I walked the four blocks back to Billeting and checked first to see if I had any messages. The light was blinking, letting me know I had at least one message. I flopped down and played them back. Her father had called me twice. And that was it. No Kevin! I put on my pajamas and went to bed, where I cried myself to sleep. The next morning, I woke up at seven. The light was blinking again. I checked, but it was Jazmine's father again. I called him back and gave him all of the information I had regarding our daughter. He said he wasn't going to be able to come to visit her because he was on a Temporary Tour of Duty (TDY) in San Diego again. "Kiss her for me, and tell her that her Daddy loves her and would be there if he could." Yeah, whatever!

I took a shower and got dressed to head back to the hospital. A nurse was giving Jazmine a sponge bath when I got to the hospital.

"Good morning, Momma! She had a little accident and threw up on herself. But she is nice and clean now. Did you get breakfast? If not, go get something to eat and hurry back so you can be here when the doctor makes his rounds."

I kissed Jazmine on the forehead and went to the Mess Hall to get a breakfast sandwich and a coffee to go. The doctor was just walking into the room when I got back to the hospital. There were several students with him. He explained to me what effect Kawasaki's disease has on the body. It causes internal swelling of the blood vessels and can cause damage to the heart, which is why they were monitoring it carefully. Her legs, arms, and hands were swollen, and she continued to have a fever. They were hoping she would eat something for breakfast, even if it were just Jell-O or maybe some applesauce.

The whole time he was explaining to me what the disease does, and the prognosis, I was listening intently, but also wishing I were not alone.

That's when I decided to suck it up and call my birth mother. After Jazmine when to sleep that afternoon, I went back to my room and called my mother's house. She didn't answer the phone, but I left her a message. I didn't know if she would be glad to hear from me, or if she would even call me back. Just as I was about to lay down for a minute, the phone rang.

"Hello?"

"Hey, baby! It is so good to hear your voice!" my mother said. It had been at least fifteen years or more.

I told her that I was in San Antonio at the military hospital at Fort Sam Houston with my eighteen-month-old daughter, and I was all alone. I didn't know how far away she lived, but I hoped she could come and see me. She promised she would come on the weekend. I thanked her, and we hung up.

I was excited; I called my father.

"Hey, Daddy, how are you? I meant to have called before now. I've just been so overwhelmed." I knew he blamed himself for my daughter getting sick, but he wasn't at fault. It was just something that happened, and I don't know why and wasn't going to question it. I assured him that he wasn't at fault.

"Is her father out there with you?"

"No, just me. He's on TDY."

"That's BS! They would let him out of that if he told them that his child was in the ICU fighting to survive. That's pure BS! I'm going to get a ticket and get out there. Where are you?"

I gave him all of the information, and he called back later to tell me that he was going to be coming out the next day.

"Thank you, Daddy!" I said tearfully.

I wished that I could see Kevin, or at least hear his voice. I called Sherita again.

"Sherita, what did Kevin say when you told him that I had to come to San Antonio because my baby is sick?"

"He didn't say anything. Look, I was trying not to have to tell you this. But Kevin ain't no good. He's done this same thing to several of my friends. I didn't want you two to even meet, but Wayne insisted we invite him over. Kevin is a dog, girl! He is a dog. And he ain't thinking about you! You said he told you he loves you? Bull! Kevin don't love nobody but Kevin!" she said spitefully. I didn't believe anything she said. There was no way that man was trying to play me. Kevin loved me! Of that, I was sure.

"What's Wayne's phone number at work?"

"Why you want to know my husband's job number?" she snapped.

"I want to talk to him. He knows Kevin better than you do."

"Hell no! I ain't giving you his number! If you want to waste your time hunting down a nigga that ain't even thinking about you, go right ahead, but you are going to leave us out of it!"

I hung up on her crazy behind! She was lying! Kevin wasn't like that!

I had been played by men before, and they all acted the same way. I knew when I was being played! Kevin was not playing me!

I remembered he had given me an envelope and told me not to open it until I was home. I searched through my luggage until I found it. I sat on the bed and turned on the light. I opened the envelope and took out the card. Several one-hundred-dollar bills fell from the card! Shocked, I picked up the crisp bills and counted them. There were sixteen one-hundred-dollar bills!

I called Sherita back.

"Kevin gave me a card and told me not to open it until I got home. I just opened it, and there are sixteen one-hundred-dollar bills inside. If he didn't love me, why would he give me sixteen hundred dollars?"

"That's all he thought a weekend with you is worth! Damn, girl!" she laughed.

I hung up on her!

I had to find this man. I called directory assistance again. I tried to explain to the operator how important it was that I reach him. I lied and said his daughter was in the ICU. But she still refused to give me his number.

"Well, can you call him and tell him and give him this number?"

"No, ma'am, I can't. There has to be another way for you to reach him."

The only other way was to talk to Wayne, and Sherita was not going to give me his number. Why? Because if I had the phone number, I could call Kevin myself since he and Wayne worked together. What a miserable woman Sherita was! I called her all kinds of evil names before going back to the hospital to be with my daughter. The next morning when my dad arrived, he caught me by surprise. I was sitting on the side of Jazmine's bed, trying to convince her that she should try just one spoonful of oatmeal, but she wasn't having any of it. Her lips were pressed together tightly.

She spotted someone entering the room, and a wide smile came across her face. I turned to see who she saw.

"Daddy!" I squealed. I hugged him tightly, and he went to her bed.

"Pumpkin! How are you doing?" He kissed her on the forehead, and she held him firmly.

"Poppa is so sorry you got sick. I love you so much, and I hope you get better real soon," he said, holding her.

"Look, Poppa," she said, raising her arm so he could see her IV. He held her arm and tried to explain that she needed it there because it was giving her some good medicine to help her get better. She was looking into his eyes, and just like that, she was convinced it wasn't a bad thing.

"You look tired, sweetie. Why don't you go take a nap? I'm here now," he said.

I kissed Jazmine on her forehead and hugged Daddy. I walked to the Mess Hall, got a sandwich, and went back to my room. After I ate, I took a shower and tried to get to sleep. All I could think about was Kevin. I could feel his touch. I could hear his voice and his silly laugh. I had it bad! Yet it still felt good.

11

I EVENTUALLY FELL INTO A RESTLESS sleep. I dreamed of the weekend that turned into a week with this wonderful man. To hear Sherita telling me that Kevin used women and that he had done this to several of her friends - I knew it was a lie. First of all, her evil behind didn't have any friends because she kept people at bay. I didn't believe her at all. After dozing, I woke up crying a few minutes later. I got the card and read it again. He loved me. I was convinced of that. Kevin loved me!

I went back to sleep with the card pressed against my body. By the time I woke up, it was afternoon! I was exhausted even after having that five-hour nap. I took a warm shower, got dressed, and went to the Mess Hall to get an early dinner before it got crowded. I got an extra plate for my dad and went back to the hospital. He had removed his shoes and was lying in Jazmine's bed with her curled up beside him; her IV arm thrown across his chest.

I sat down in the recliner and went right back to sleep. I was sleeping well when the doctor was tapping my hand.

"We have some good news. Her temperature is back to normal! And the swelling has gone down in her extremities. She is looking good. I want her to get up for about ten minutes each morning and evening and just take a walk around the corridor. Walk along with her at her pace. No rushing. I just want to get the blood pumping. Encourage her to drink plenty of liquids. Right now, we are not worried about sugar overload, okay. So, we have apple juice, grape juice, ginger ale, and of course, water. Any questions?" I was about to ask one when my dad asked him about the foods she could eat.

"We are trying to get her to eat soft food: oatmeal, Jell-O, apple sauce, yogurt. But in the next couple of days, we will try mashed potatoes, cream corn, that sort of food. You guys hang in there," he said and moved on to the next patient. I looked at Daddy and smiled.

"Prayer works, Baby Girl!" he reminded me.

Later that evening, Daddy and I went for a walk along the Riverwalk. I decided to tell him about my visit to Hampton.

"Do you believe that he was lying to you?" he asked.

"Daddy, he gave me sixteen hundred dollars inside of a card. He looked me in my face and told me how much he wanted me to come back to Hampton. He was going to get me and Jazmine an apartment. He didn't say he was going to get "us", as in me and him an apartment; but us as in me and my daughter. He meant what he said, Daddy. I know that for a fact. I just don't know how to contact him. I've tried to remember that phone number, and I just can't."

That was indeed a fact. I didn't, for one minute, believe Kevin wasn't telling me the truth. I also knew if I could just speak to Wayne, I would get the information I needed about Kevin. Unfortunately, that didn't happen.

Finally, I made one more effort to reach Sherita. This time, I would try a different approach.

"Hi, Sherita, how are you doing?"

"Hey! You sound much better. It must be some good news! How is my baby doing?"

"Yes, I was calling to tell you the good news. Jazmine is doing better. Her temperature is back to normal. The swelling in her extremities has gone down. She has a twinkle in her eyes again. She's looking good, Sherita."

"That's good. I've been praying for her."

"Have you seen Kevin lately?" I asked once she sounded cheerful enough.

"We saw him this weekend when he came over here with this big butt, ugly chick. I couldn't believe that he would bring a woman to my house after he had treated you like crap. I told you he ain't no good."

"He had another woman with him?" I asked, shocked.

"You were the only one who thought he was a good man!" she said, laughing.

Well, that didn't go as I planned. I was now sorry I even called her. She had more practice at being evil than I thought. However, what if she was telling the truth? I didn't want to believe it! But what if?

I didn't have long to think about that because my birth mother called me later that day.

"I'm in the lobby!" she said.

I put my shoes on and took the stairs down instead of the elevator. I didn't know if I even remembered what she looked like. However, as soon as I entered the lobby, I knew right away she was my mother. She was crying. She pulled me and held me securely in her arms. She pulled back and looked at my face.

"Look at you! Oh, my God! You are a woman! You are so beautiful!" she cried. I led her to the elevator, and we went up to my room. I stepped to the side, allowing her to enter first.

"Have a seat! Did you drive over?" I asked.

I had no idea where she lived. All I knew was that she had married a GI, and no one had heard from her again until she wrote me a letter a few years ago, and the address was a Texas address. Aunt Gladys threw the letter away, but she told my father about it. I wished I had read it so I could see what she wanted to tell me.

We sat down on the sofa, facing each other, and started talking at the same time.

"You go ahead," I offered.

"I was so surprised to hear from you. I thought you hated me. I've been writing to you since you were a little girl and never heard back from you, so I thought you hated me."

"Where were you mailing the letters?" I had never gotten one letter from her!

"I only had your aunt's address. Are you saying you never got them? I sent money to you every month."

"I have never gotten a letter or any money!"

"We can talk about that later. I want you to meet my baby." I didn't want to hear bad news, not with all of the good news going on right now.

We walked to the hospital and got to Jazmine's room, but it was empty. I panicked, thinking something had happened to my daughter. Crying, I ran to the nurse's station.

"She's in the playroom," the nurse said.

I breathed a sigh of relief and went to the playroom.

She was the only child there. She had taken several dolls and placed them in chairs around a table. She was reading to them from *Good Night Moon*.

"Momma! Come and sit down. Let me read to you," she said.

I said I wanted her to meet someone first. I introduced her to my mother. She hugged her, but she was more interested in getting us to sit down at the table so she could read to us from her favorite book. I didn't know if I could sit in a chair that small, and I knew, for a fact, my mother couldn't. Her butt was a tad bit bigger than mine. We sat on the sofa, and Jazmine pulled the chair around to sit in front of us. I had read this book to her so many times that she knew it by heart.

She "read" the first page, and it caught my mother off guard.

"She knows how to read?" she asked.

"You have to be quiet now. This is a good book," Jazmine said, sounding just like me.

It was good to hear her talking, laughing, and having a good time. We played with her until she started getting tired. I took her back to her room and helped her get comfortable in the bed. In ten minutes, she was sound asleep.

My mother and I went to the Mess Hall to have lunch.

"You never answered me. Did you drive here?" I asked.

"Yes, I did. It's only about an hour and a half drive from Killeen here," she said.

"Are you still married?" I asked when I didn't see her wedding rings.

"No. I've been divorced for about eleven years."

"Why didn't you come back to New York?"

"I had a good job here. My home is paid for. I wasn't in New York long enough to consider it home. What are you going to do when Jazmine gets released? Are you going back to New York?"

"I don't know what I'm going to do. I don't have anywhere to go." I couldn't very well go to Hampton now that Kevin may have moved on. I didn't have the energy to get hurt again.

12

"**YOU CAN COME STAY WITH** me. I have a couple of spare bedrooms. That is if you want to. I would love to have you," my mother said.

"I would like to go live with you. Thank you," I said.

Two weeks later, when my daughter was to be released, I had to call Daddy and tell him that I was going to live in Texas with my mother.

"If that's what you want to do, do it. You're an adult. Ain't nobody got nothing negative to say about it. If they do, let me know," he said.

"Well, you know, Aunt Gladys!"

"You are twenty-five-years-old! That makes you a grown woman. If your mother invited you to come to her house, that's your prerogative to go. Don't make me start cussing!" he said, laughing.

"You're not angry?"

"Angry about what? She's your mother!"

Since I had Daddy's approval, I didn't care what anyone else would say. The day Jazmine was released, my mother was with us to drive us back to Killeen. The hospital gave us a car seat since I didn't have one with me.

Once we got to my mother's house, she led us inside. It was a split-level style house with a beautifully manicured yard. There were colorful hedges that lined the entire front of the house.

We went up the stairs and entered the living room. "Come on in," she said. She had a large circular sectional that took up one mirrored wall. She had pictures of me when I was a little girl on the wall by the two matching chairs. A fireplace was against the other wall, and there were more pictures of me, and some of her over the fireplace.

"Come, let me show you the bedrooms. I have two empty rooms; you can pick which one you want. Only one of them has a bathroom. The other one is small; I've been using it as a den. We can move the furniture out of there and put it in the storage unit out back. But you can decide," she said nervously.

I followed her down the hallway toward the first bedroom. It was small, and I didn't think it would be enough room for both my baby and me. We followed her back the way we came. The next bedroom was at the opposite end of the house. That bedroom had a queen-size bed, a dresser, and a large cabinet that held books on one wall. A chair and desk were there as well. The bathroom was a nice size also.

"This one is good," I said.

"I'll bring you some bedding, and y'all go on and get comfortable. Make yourselves at home," she said, leaving the room. She returned with a beautiful comforter set still in the package and fresh sheets. After getting the bed made up, and putting our clothes in the walk-in closet, I laid Jazmine down for her nap. My mother was in the kitchen preparing dinner.

"I thought I would make a big dinner since you're here, fried chicken, collards, candied yams, cornbread, and some potato salad. How does that sound?" she asked.

"Amazing!" I replied. I offered to help, but she told me to just keep her company. I pulled the chair from the table and sat down. She went to the cabinet and got down a wineglass, poured some wine into it, and filled her glass back up. She had changed into shorts and an oversized T-shirt. An apron was around her waist, and she wore flipflops. She was nervous, and I could see from where I was seated that she didn't know what to say to me.

"I used to live in New Mexico. I married a guy who joined the Air Force," I said.

She turned to look at me, "Really? So close but so far away. How long were you out there?"

"I was there for almost four years. We got divorced, but I stayed on for a little while, then went back to New York. I stayed with Aunt Gladys."

"Gladys! Me and Gladys were like sisters. We were tighter than a fat lady's pantyhose. Yes, we were!" she chuckled.

"Really? I didn't think Aunt Gladys had any friends," I said, laughing.

"She is a trip, ain't she? Gladys was fine with me until your father, and I got serious. She didn't think I was good enough for your Dad. I was too dark. Too short. Too country. Child! Gladys was a mess!"

I watched as she cut up the chicken and washed it. Her greens were simmering on the stove, and I could smell the ham she had placed in the pot. She began frying the chicken. After it all was in the frying pan, she cut up the potatoes and made her potato salad.

"Are you hungry?" she asked.

"I am now!" I said.

"We're going to be eating in a few minutes. If you don't mind, can you get the table set? Let the baby sleep, and we can talk."

She had a large china cabinet and motioned that I was to get those dishes. I set the table and poured myself another glass of wine. She filled the platters with the chicken, the greens, potato salad, candied yams, and the hot cornbread. Everything smelled amazing.

"Let's thank God. You want to do it?" she asked.

I bowed my head and thanked God for the food, for my mother, and her hospitality. She was smiling when I raised my head. She held up her glass, and I clicked mine against hers.

13

"YOU ARE SO BEAUTIFUL, BABY. You're not leaving behind a broken heart?" my mom asked.

"Right before Jazmine got sick, I had met a guy one weekend when I went to Hampton to visit some friends of mine. That weekend turned into a week. A wonderful week! He gave me his phone number, but I didn't write it down because I can remember numbers. Well, I thought I could. But by the time I got back home and found out my baby was sick, I just couldn't remember the number. I called my friend, who lives in Hampton. She told me he was just using me. I don't think that is the truth. But I didn't know how to get in touch with him. She won't give me her husband's phone number... I loved this guy. He loved me. I know that for a fact. He gave me sixteen hundred dollars inside a card. I wish I knew how to get in touch with him."

"Give me his name, and I will see if a friend of mine on base can run it and see how to contact him," she said. She handed me a pad and pencil to write Kevin's information on. I felt so much better knowing this might be ending, and I could get to Hampton.

That night, as I lay in bed after my baby had gone to sleep, I thought about Kevin and the wonderful time we had together. No one would ever be able to convince me it meant nothing. I knew, in my heart, it did, and I held on to that.

The next day, my mother called to tell me that her friend tried to look for Kevin, but he had moved off the base. His address was not known, and his phone number was unlisted.

"If he ever applies for a VA loan, we will find him then," she said.

I wanted him now. Not years from now! A voice was telling me that I had tried everything I knew to try, but I had to let it go now. It was over. I cried myself to sleep every night. I knew it was time to get a job. I went to the employment office and registered for a job. I didn't want to work on the base. No more bartending for me. I didn't want to be around any more men!

I was a secretary in New York, and that was the kind of job I wanted here. I wanted a nine-to-five so that I could be there for my child in the evenings. Besides, I had to ride public transportation, since I no longer had a car.

Two weeks later, I was hired by a law firm downtown. My mother was friends with a Korean lady who lived next door who agreed to watch Jazmine. I went over to LeAnn's house to meet her, bringing Jazmine with me. Her home was spotless; she didn't smoke or have any pets. She had a little boy named Liam who was in school during the day, and her husband was in the military.

Every day I dropped my daughter off at LeAnn's house and caught the bus downtown. I had to walk three blocks to get to the law firm of Dudley and Watts. I usually wore sneakers and changed into my heels once I got there. I was one of two African American women in the firm. The other secretary, Mrs. White, was the secretary for Mr. Watts. I was the secretary for Mr. Dudley and the other attorneys. Therefore, my entire day was busy, answering the phones, typing up briefs, and memos, filing things at the courthouse. Most days, I never got to put my heels on and keep them on. After work was over, I walked the three blocks to the bus station and went home. I picked up Jazmine and usually fixed us something to eat and was laying across my bed watching TV by the time my mother got home.

She never invited me to join her as she watched TV, though sometimes, I could hear we were watching the same program.

One night, I decided to make the first move. I didn't want to feel like a boarder in her home. She was my mother, and I wanted to get to know her.

"I see you like Dallas and Dynasty, too. Would you like some popcorn and wine?" I asked.

"I love this show. Alexis is my girl! And JR! Lord, he is going to mess around, and someone is going to blow his brains out! Yes, popcorn and wine sound nice," she said.

When the popcorn finished popping, I was going to put it in two separate bowls, but changed my mind and put it all in one bowl.

I poured us two glasses of wine and came back in to join her.

"The baby's sleeping?" she asked.

"Yeah, she's knocked out!" I said, laughing.

"You haven't met any of your coworkers?"

"Yes, I've met all of them. That is one busy place, Mom. I hardly ever get to wear my heels!"

"Aren't you tired of sitting in this house all the time? Why don't you go out and meet folks your age?"

"I don't know if I want to meet anyone,"

"Well, you don't need to stay cooped up in this house, either.

You're young, smart, and beautiful. There's another guy out there, sweetie. You have to trust someone else."

I knew she was right. I was still in love with Kevin, and I was holding out hope that somehow, I would find him.

My mother didn't believe me. One Friday evening, she came home with a big bag of cleaned and prepped fish to fry.

"I have some friends coming over around 7:30. Can you help me get this food cooked? I'm frying up some fish, making some stewed potatoes and onions. I probably make some cornbread and string beans. The bag of string beans is on the table. If you could snap them for me? I'll go ahead and get this fish washed to fry."

I assumed her friends were female. At 7:30, the doorbell rang, and when I answered it, there were two very handsome African American men standing there. The one who rang the bell was a bit taller than me. The other one, as he stepped inside, was tall, had broad shoulders, and was handsome.

"I smell food! And it is smelling amazing!" he said.

"Come on in, fellows. Let me introduce you to my daughter. Dedra, this is Stewart and Cobb. Y'all, this is my daughter; we call her Dee Dee. Tell me again what your first names are," she said, looking up at the tallest one.

"My name is Samuel Stewart; my boy, Richard Cobb. Everyone calls me, Sam," he said.

"It's nice meeting you both," I said. I thought my mother had good taste. Even though Sam Stewart could be her son, I assumed, for some reason, he was her man.

While she showed them to the living room and offered each a beer, which they declined, I continued setting the table. I put three plates on the table. She noticed and asked me why I wasn't eating.

"I ate already, Mom." She waved her hand for me to come to her.

"Please, eat with us. C'mon baby," she pleaded.

I put another plate on the table, and we all sat down to eat.

"Dee Dee, baby, since you say such lovely prayers, can you say the blessing?"

I knew it wouldn't look good to refuse, so I said the blessing, and we began passing the platters and bowls of food around. "Everything looks and smells amazing. I know it's going to be good, Mrs. Andrews," Sam said. When he called her Mrs. Andrews, I knew for sure he wasn't her man. Was she trying to play matchmaker? Yes! That is exactly what she was doing. I decided I would eat quickly, excuse myself, and go to bed. However, Sam began engaging me in conversation.

"How do you like Killeen? I know it must be a culture shock coming from New York," he said.

"I haven't been anywhere to be able to compare the two cities," I replied.

"What do you like to do for fun?"

"I have a daughter. So, between work and her, I'm pretty busy and don't have much time for fun things."

"Well, maybe I can take you out sometime; show you around." I didn't want to be rude. I just smiled and thanked him.

I don't know how it happened. While I was cleaning the kitchen, Sam volunteered to help me. I handed him the dishcloth, and I began putting the leftover food in plastic containers. He was at the sink, washing the dishes. I began rinsing them off and putting them in the dish drainer.

"Are you always this quiet?" Sam asked.

"Just until I get to know you."

Though I said that, it wasn't an invitation for him to think I wanted to get to know him better, but that is exactly how he took it. Then he asked me out that weekend.

"Can I let you know later?" That sounded like I wanted to have his phone number! I was batting two for zero!

After we washed and dried the dishes and pots, I put some lotion on my hands and offered him some. He held out his hands, and though I didn't look up at him, I knew he was looking at me. Without thinking that I was giving lotion to a grown man, and not my child, I began rubbing the lotion in on his hands.

"I'm so sorry! I always have to rub the lotion in for my daughter. I just ... "

"It's okay. It is only lotion," he said and continued holding out his hands for me to rub the lotion in.

We joined my mom and Richard in the living room; he sat on the loveseat with me.

"What were you two giggling about?" Mom asked.

I didn't even realize we had been giggling, so I let him answer her. "We were just getting to know one another better," he replied.

Around ten, they both stood up to leave.

"It was very nice meeting you, Dedra. I hope to hear from you again soon," Sam said. My mother had fixed them both plates to take with them. I gave them their food. Mom and I stood on the porch, waving until they got into their car.

I was tired, and it was past my bedtime by then. We came back inside, and she playfully popped me on the arm. "You go, girl!" she teased.

"Now, don't go getting your hopes up, okay. I already told you I am not interested in getting involved with anyone right now."

"So, what do you think about Sam?" she asked before they had even backed out of the driveway good!

"He seems to be a nice guy. But as I said before, my heart is in love with another man. And I hope to one day find him." I went to bed, leaving her standing there.

The next day at work, the receptionist came to my office, carrying a large bouquet of colorful flowers. She was smiling broadly and handed them to me.

"For me?" I asked, surprised.

I read the card and saw they were from Sam. I put them in a vase and placed them on my desk. I didn't have to ask how he found out where I worked, that was my Mom's doing. When I got off from work that evening, I put my sneakers on and headed out to walk the three blocks in the Texas heat to my bus stop. As soon as I opened the door to leave, there stood Sam about to come in.

"What are you doing here?" I asked.

"I came to give you a ride home," he replied.

"Sam, that is very nice of you. But I told you, I am not interested in getting involved in a relationship."

"Relationship? Who said anything about a relationship? I am offering a beautiful woman a ride home. Certainly, a ride home in a nice air-conditioned car is better than a hot, funky bus?" He laughed.

"As a friend?"

"Sure, as a friend. No more than that."

After settling into his nice air-conditioned Jaguar, he asked how my day went.

"I'm tired! If I could, I would take a vacation! That's how my day went."

"If you could go anywhere you want, where would you want to go?"

I didn't even have to think about that answer. "The Bahamas!" I had to sigh, just thinking about it.

When we pulled into my mom's driveway, I thanked him for the ride and opened the door.

"I'll see you tomorrow, same time," he said.

"Thank you, but you don't have to give me a ride home."

"I know that. I want to. See you tomorrow."

I walked next door and picked up Jazmine, who was watching me from the window as usual. She was always anxious to tell me about her day, and I was always anxious to hear about it. We went to the bedroom, and I began changing clothes while she talked non-stop. They had gone to the park, the zoo, and to get pizza. She said she hadn't taken a nap, and I was glad to hear that because I was tired.

I gave her a juice cup and turned on the TV to her favorite cartoon – *Tom & Jerry*. Within fifteen minutes, she was snoring softly beside me. I soon was sleeping as well.

The smell of taco meat woke me up. I splashed water on my face and went to the kitchen, where my mom was making tacos.

"Hey, baby! Grab a beer from the fridge and have a seat. How was work?"

I got a beer and sat down to talk with her.

"You got home early tonight," she said.

"I got a ride home with Sam."

She turned to look at me and raised her bottle of beer.

"Mom, I told you, we are just friends. I am not interested in a relationship with him, and he is happy with that." "Okay! Okay! Set the table for me," she said, laughing.

I could tell by the grin on her face she was hoping for more.

14

ONE SUNDAY MORNING, AFTER my mom had gone to church, the phone rang. Lo and behold, it was Aunt Gladys. I had no idea she even had my mother's phone number.

"How did you get this number?" I asked.

"I've had your mom's number for fifteen years. Where is she? Put her on the phone," she said.

"She went to church. Wait a minute! What do you mean you've had her number for fifteen years? All the times I wanted to contact her, you had her number and never offered to give it to me?" I was shocked.

"It wasn't my place to give it to you!"

"Really? Whose place was it then? I can't believe this! I'll tell her to call you when she gets in. Bye!" I hung up, furious.

I called Dad. "Daddy, did you know Aunt Gladys had my mom's number for fifteen years?"

"What are you talking about? Who told you that?"

"She just told me that! And she said she didn't give it to me because it wasn't her place!"

"Let me call her! I will call you right back!"

I sat by the phone, steaming mad, waiting for my father to call me back. Finally, the phone rang.

"She told me that they talked two or three times a week for the past fifteen years! All of these years, I've been wondering where your mother was and to think my sister knew all along and never said anything! I can't believe this crap! Gladys messed up this time! I'm ticked off. Let me call you when I calm down!" he said before hanging up.

Aunt Gladys knew how much I wanted to talk to my mother, and she hid this from my father and me. I could not believe she would be this cruel; this evil! I was still seething when my mother got home from church three hours later.

"Mom, Aunt Gladys called you. She said she's known where you've been for at least fifteen years. Is that true?"

"Gladys has always known where I've been." She sat down, removed her heels, and then her hat. She laid it on the sofa beside her.

"Mom, please, tell me what happened. Why did you leave my father?"

"Can you get me a glass of water first?" she asked. I got her the water and sat down on the sofa beside her, facing her.

"Gladys told me that your father had gotten another woman pregnant. She said your dad was in love with this woman. I asked your father about it. He denied it. He had no idea what I was talking about. I didn't believe him because Gladys told me he was going to deny it. She showed me a photo of your father with a woman. They were hugging. I was so hurt, baby. I just left. I knew he would take good care of you, so I just left. I didn't run off with a man! I left because your father had ripped out my heart and was lying to me," she cried.

"Do you still have that photo?" I asked because I knew how she saved everything.

"It's down in that cabinet—a red photo album. In the back, the last page," she said, wiping the tears away.

I got up and looked for the photo album. I handed it to her. She opened it up and handed me the photo without looking at it.

I took the photo from her shaking hands.

"This is Daddy's cousin, June! This isn't his girlfriend!"

My mom sat up, "What?" she asked, shocked.

"This is my Cousin June. This isn't his girlfriend! Why would Aunt Gladys tell that lie?" I knew she was shady, but this was too shocking! She broke up our family! Why?

"Baby, let me handle it, okay? Let me do it. There is no need for you to get caught up in all of this. I will talk to your father, okay?" She got up wearily, took her hat and shoes, and went to her bedroom.

I left it alone because she asked me to, but I would never forgive Aunt Gladys for what she did!

⁓

On Friday, when Sam came to pick me up, he asked if I wanted to go to the zoo before going home.

"I have to get home to pick up my daughter," I said.

"Not today, you don't. Your mom is picking her up. C'mon! Don't you want to see the lions and tigers and bears? Please," he said, begging like a little kid.

I agreed to go with him to the zoo. I put my sneakers on when we got there and got out of the car.

"Why is it that a beautiful woman like you don't want a relationship?" he asked as we walked along.

"I fell in love with someone before I came to Texas. I haven't gotten him out of my system. It wouldn't be fair to enter another relationship until I am sure that I'm not in love with him anymore."

"What happened, if you don't mind me asking?"

"I have a niche. I can remember numbers without writing them down. I still remember the combination of my locker in junior high. Well, I told him to just give me his phone number because I was positive that I would remember it. When I got back to New York from a trip seeing him, my baby was very sick. That's how we ended up here in Texas. I tried to call him the night I got back, after everything was quiet, you know. But I couldn't remember the number. I called directory assistance. The next day, I called some friends of mine that knew him, but the wife answered the phone. She said some really cruel things to me. Anyway, I couldn't find his number. I tried everything I could think of." "Oh, that's the guy your mom had me try to locate. He must have been very special."

"He was. I thought he was. I don't know."

"I apologize on his behalf. Maybe it was just miscommunication. Maybe your friend never told him you were trying to find him. Maybe he is everything you thought he was. Just don't write the rest of us off, okay?"

After we left the zoo, he took me to his favorite Mexican restaurant. It was a bit crowded because it was Friday night, but after an hour, we were shown to our table.

I ordered a frozen margarita as soon as the waitress came by. Sam was driving, so he had to order ice tea.

"What about you? Have you ever been married?" I asked.

"Yes, I have. I got married, and it lasted for about two years. I left to go to Japan, and she didn't want to quit her job and come with me. We talked all the time on the phone, she wrote to me and sent cards. She left one thing out. She had moved another dude into my house. When I came back stateside, she had a little girl about one-year-old. I was gone for three years! That pretty much ended that right there."

"Wow! She sounds like she's cut from the same cloth as my ex-husband," I said, laughing.

"You've been married before, too?" he asked.

"Yes. It lasted for almost two years. He was seeing another woman, who made it her mission in life to call and harass me constantly. I got sick of it all and told her she could have him."

After our drinks came, we ordered our food. We were having so much fun talking and getting to know one another; I lost track of time. It was almost 8:30!

"I have to call my mom. I'll be right back."

I went to the payphone and called my mom.

"Girl, we are doing just fine. You have a good evening. Don't worry about us. We are playing dolls and watching this funny cartoon – *Tom & Jerry*. Have some fun."

After I told him that I didn't have to rush home, he asked if I wanted to catch a free concert.

"What kind of concert is free? Whose performing?"

"Several groups. It's for the officers and their families. Seriously! Let me see who all is there," he said, removing a ticket from his wallet.

"The Temptations and the Four Tops," he said, smiling.

I reached for the tickets because I could not believe the Temptations and the Four Tops were performing a free concert in Killeen, Texas. He was right!

We ended up at the park, sitting on the ground on a scratchy blanket, watching a free concert.

We were so close to the stage I could have spit on the shoes of one of the Temptations. People were up dancing or trying to dance. I didn't think I would, but I was enjoying the concert. The Four Tops went on last. When they sang the song, "I Believe in You and Me," Sam asked me to dance. I took his hand, and we stood to dance. I could tell he was looking down at me. I kept my head lowered. He smelled so good! He gently pulled me closer to him.

I did look up at him. He smiled, and I smiled back. I rested my head against his chest. He held me, his hands at the small of my back. Just as the song was ending, he tilted my chin up and kissed me.

We held hands walking to the car, neither of us saying anything until we got inside the vehicle.

"Did you enjoy the concert?" he asked.

"I did! It was very nice. Thanks for inviting me."

As usual, he opened the car door and helped me get in, then he went around and got in. We laughed and talked about the concert and the people we saw trying to dance.

"I'm only going to say this; some folks were not in line to get rhythm when it was being passed out! Did you see the couple with the camouflage on? Oh, my goodness!" I said, laughing.

"I like your moves," he said, smiling.

"I like your moves, too."

I sauntered in the house to find my mom sitting in the living room, the TV on, and my daughter lying with her head in her lap.

"What are you two doing up?" I asked.

"We were waiting up for you," she replied.

I sat down and threw my head back.

"I had a good time tonight."

"Then why are you home so early?"

"I didn't have that good of a time. We are just friends, Mom." I reminded her for the hundredth time.

"Okay, whatever! Things have certainly changed since I went out on a date with a man."

"See, this wasn't a date. It was two friends going to see a concert. It would have been the same if I had gone out with a friend that is a female."

"Girl, come get this baby so that I can go to bed. I done heard it all!" she said, laughing.

I put Jazmine in the bed, washed my makeup off, and put on my pajamas. When the phone rang, I knew it was probably Sam. I was glad I had gotten a phone for my bedroom, so I didn't disturb my mother.

"Hi there," he said.

"Didn't I just see you?" I teased him.

"Yes, you did. But I wanted to thank you for hanging out with me tonight."

"You are certainly welcome. I had a good time. Thank you, too."

"I was wondering if you wanted to do something tomorrow. We, I mean, you, you can bring your daughter. She must be bored being in the house all the time, too."

"Okay, that will be nice. I will talk to you tomorrow."

"Good night, my friend."

"Good night, my friend."

What I was starting to feel for him was no longer "friendship." I enjoyed being with him. I liked the way he made me feel, and I liked the way he wanted to include my daughter in our plans.

15

AS WE WALKED PAST EACH CAGE at the zoo the next day, Jazmine sitting on Sam's shoulders, I reached for his hand. It seemed to startle him. He looked down at me, kissed my hand, and smiled.

"Y'all want to come by my place for lunch? I make a mean tuna sandwich," Sam said, laughing.

"Sure, I can eat a tuna sandwich," I replied.

Sam didn't live that far from where Mom lived. He lived in a beautiful townhouse community. Sam led us into his den, which was right next to his kitchen. Jazmine was sleepy; I lay her down on his sofa and went to the kitchen and sat on the stool by his island.

"Can I get you something to drink?" he asked.

"Apple juice, please," I said.

He poured both of us a glass of juice and set my glass down in front of me.

He began talking in a fake French accent as he put the things he needed to make the tuna fish on the island. He put two eggs in a pot of water to boil and placed it on the burner.

He was so goofy!

"I have to put in my secret ingredient, so you need to turn your head," he said.

"What secret ingredient? I asked.

"Turn your head!"

I turned my head; I could see his reflection in the mirror on the wall. He went to the cabinet and removed a container of Old Bay Seasoning. He sprinkled some in the tuna and put it back.

"I saw that! I got your secret ingredient! I got your secret ingredient!" I sang. He came from behind the island and put his arms around me!

"Now I must chop you up and put you in the freezer!" he said, making me laugh.

We stopped laughing. He was still holding me; it seemed the only thing to do was kiss him.

When I pulled away, he licked his lips and smiled.

"Are friends supposed to kiss?" he asked.

"I couldn't help myself."

Things changed for us with that kiss. We went from being friends just hanging out together to lovers. It had been a year, and I hadn't heard one word from Kevin. I knew it was over for us. I allowed myself to move on.

My mother would have turned flips if she could have; she was just that happy for me. I was happy also, and glad we took our time to get to know one another.

Sam told me about his father, who lived in North Carolina. His mother had passed away when he was in basic training. His father had never remarried, though he had been looking for the perfect woman. He hadn't found her yet, so he remained single. He was a college professor and was going to retire in a couple of years, if not earlier. I wanted to meet him.

I had planned to visit my dad before the weather got cold in New York, so we decided to go to Greensboro first to meet Sam's dad first.

SAM, JAZMINE, AND I flew to Greensboro, North Carolina so that I could meet his father, and he could meet mine in New York. The first stop, though, was Greensboro. His father was waiting for us at the airport to take us to Winston Salem, where he lived.

Sam had spoken highly of his dad, and we had talked on the phone a couple of times, so we were not strangers. His nickname was Big Sam. Because of that, I expected to see a man larger than Sam. I didn't know he could have been bigger because Sam was six feet, five inches tall. A man who was just an inch above six feet met us. He was a retired professor at the local college and carried himself with dignity and flair. He was what folks called smooth. I saw where Sam got his good looks and his charisma. Big Sam picked us up, driving a gray and black Bentley.

Big Sam lived in a sprawling home that was now occupied by only him.

"My son keeps telling me he is going to retire here and get a place with an in-law suite for me to stay. He better not renege on that promise. I'm tired of this big, empty house!" he said.

Though he was only sixty-two, I found it hard to believe he would be satisfied living in a basement apartment, after seeing this huge house, and the three cars in the garage, but he seemed serious.

Sam and I were getting ready for bed; I asked him if his father would be satisfied living in a basement apartment.

"My dad got all of this stuff for my mom. He didn't get it for himself; trust me. Mom always felt that we had to live bigger than the next guy. My dad is a simple kind of guy. Aside from the cars, he's not like this at all.

Sam's mother had passed away seven years ago from a massive stroke. Big Sam had put the house on the market twice, and then changed his mind a couple of weeks after the sign went up.

"I believe he means it this time," he said.

He certainly knew his father better than I did.

We spent a week with his father in Winston Salem, before flying to New York to see my dad. My father lived nothing like Big Sam. He lived in a modest one-bedroom apartment in a refurbished brownstone in Bedford/Stuyvesant and was a retired butcher. He didn't even own a car. What they did have in common was their flare.

I knew when they met that they would get along well together.

Since we were in New York, I thought we would do some things that tourists do. We went to see the Statue of Liberty, the museums, Chinatown, Penn Station, Times Square, and Harlem.

We were gone for two weeks, sharing a week with each of our fathers. When we returned to Texas, Sam asked me to marry him.

I asked if I could think about it. "Sure, yes," he said, sounding a bit disappointed.

I had to try one last time to find Kevin. I called directory assistance to see if, by chance, his phone number was now listed, but it was still private. I then called Sherita. I hadn't spoken to her in over a year.

"Look what the cat dragged up!" she said once she recognized my voice—same old Sherita.

"How are you? I asked, ignoring her comment.

"We are fine. How are you?"

"I'm good. How is your family?"

"Everyone is fine. Well, physically, everyone is fine. Wayne has been busy with school. I think he is working on his second degree. I don't know what that's about. I don't know how long I'm going to be hanging around here."

I thought it was a good thing he was learning a different trade; that way, when he got out of the service, he could do whatever he wanted to do.

"Did you ever hear from Kevin?" she asked.

"No, I didn't. Anyway, I just called to say hello."

"Cool. It was good to hear from you. Take it easy." I hung up without responding.

I decided to tell Sam that I would marry him. Though I cared very much about him, I wasn't in love with him. But he was a good man, and I knew I would grow to love him. I needed someone in my life, and my baby needed a father who was present in her life. She adored Sam. It was going to be okay to say yes.

We decided to have a small ceremony and do something bigger later when he got out of the military, which he had planned to do in a couple of years.

When school started back in August, Jazmine was going to start kindergarten. We wanted to take one more vacation before school started. Instead of going out of the country, we decided to take her to Disney World in Florida.

Once we returned, my mom called to tell me that Marc had called to speak to Jazmine. We hadn't heard from him in two years. I wrote the number down and decided to call him first.

A familiar voice answered the phone when I called. This sounded like the woman who constantly called me while we were married, telling me that she was sleeping with him.

"Hello, this is Marc's ex-wife. May I speak to him, please?" I asked.

"Yes, hold on," she said. She placed the phone down and came back a few seconds later.

"He'll be here in a second."

"You must be quite happy now seeing your plan to destroy his family worked," I said before she put the phone down again.

This woman's calls had been torture. I hated her with every fiber of my being. Much like I felt about him because had he been a "good" man, he would have set her straight the first time she approached him. But he was no better.

"Hey! How's everything? I didn't think you were going to call me back," he said.

"We were out of town. Jazmine hasn't heard from you in two years. What's going on?"

"I've just been really busy. We had a baby last year."

I didn't care if they had given birth to a cow! Jazmine shouldn't have been put on the backburner because he had another child.

"Again, what is it that you want now?"

"I want to talk to my daughter!"

"And when something else comes up in your life that you deem more important, are you going to disappear from her life again until things change? She's just a little girl, Marc! She doesn't deserve to be treated that way."

"Well, I'm here now, calling to speak to my daughter!"

"I'll have her call you back on the weekend!"

What kind of parenting was that called? Each time something came up in his life that he thought was more important, he would put his child on the back burner until things cooled down? I wasn't going to let him treat my baby that way!

I took a deep breath and tried to get past the hurt. I had to call my mom!

"Mommy, Marc hasn't called Jazmine in two years. She doesn't even ask about him anymore. He told me that he and that baldheaded heffa he is living with had a baby last year, and he's been busy! What the heck is that? You get so busy that you don't have time for your daughter for two freaking years? Is he crazy?
He makes me so doggone sick!" I ranted.

"Did she talk to him?"

"She's not here right now. She went shopping with Sam; thank God because I don't want her to see me this upset."

"Are you going to let her talk to him?"

"I'm going to tell her he called to speak to her, and if she wants to call him back, she certainly can. But I'm not that mother who says, 'Call your daddy. Call your daddy.' Especially when they daddy ain't thinking about the baby until he ain't got nothing else to think about it. That's messed up!"

"Baby, try to calm down. Let him talk to her. She will see for herself what type of person he is. Don't bad mouth him to her. Please, don't do that."

Immediately, I thought of how my dad's family kept me from my mother for twenty years. She was right. I would let her speak to her father. She would see for herself what type of person he was. It wasn't my desire to hurt my daughter. I wouldn't bad mouth her father. No!

"Thank you, Mommy. I love you."

"I love you, too, darling."

Before we got ready for bed, I told Jazmine that her father, Marc, had called and wanted her to call him.

"Where is he?"

"He's still in New Mexico?"

I don't know why she asked me where he was. She put her pajamas on and got under the covers. I sat on the side of her bed and read her a book. I kissed her on the cheek, turned off the lamp, and turned on the nightlight.

"Love you, baby."

"I love you too, Mommy."

When I went downstairs, Sam was fixing a big bowl of chocolate chip, mint ice cream.

"I told Jazmine that Marc called. She asked me where was he. That was so strange," I said.

"What did you tell her?"

"I told her he is in New Mexico. She has a map, so she will see that New Mexico is right next to Texas. I don't know what I will say if she asks why he hasn't been to see her. Anyway, what are you doing with that big bowl of ice cream? Are you trying to get me fat?"

"Who said this is for you? You ain't getting none of my ice cream, woman!" He ran upstairs with me right on his heels. As I passed the light switch, I turned off the lights in the kitchen. He ran into our bedroom, slid across the wood floor in his socks, and jumped on the bed.

"You silly man!" I said as I tried to slide across the floor also.

I began tickling him as we rolled on the bed with him holding the bowl up with one arm.

He always knew how to cheer me up. Later, as I lay in his arms, I made a promise to myself that I would never talk badly about Jazmine's father to her. What I felt about him were my feelings, and I wasn't going to pass those feelings on to her.

On Sunday morning, she came into the kitchen while I was making breakfast and said she was ready to call Marc. I handed her the telephone, and she sat on the stool at the island. She dialed his number and waited for him to answer.

"I'm fine. Where have you been?" she asked. I couldn't hear his answer.

"A baby? Is it a boy or a girl?"

"I have a new father!" I nearly dropped a dozen eggs I was getting ready to cook. "His name is Sam. He is real, real, real tall. Like a giant." She giggled.

"Hold on. Mommy, he wants to talk to you," she said and held out the phone to me.

I put the phone to my ear and continued to stir my eggs.

"What's up? Did you tell her to say that?" he asked.

"Say what?"

"That you got some nigga in the house, and he's her father now?"

"That's what she said?"

"She said she has a new father!"

"No, I didn't tell her that. I wasn't listening to your conversation.
I'm trying to fix breakfast."

"Please, don't try to turn my daughter against me!"

"Are you crazy? I just said I was cooking breakfast. Your name hasn't come up in this house ever! I don't have to say anything to turn your daughter against you. Your absence from her life will do that!"

I hung up the phone and finished cooking. I was so upset that the fire coming out of my nose could have finished cooking the food.

While we were eating breakfast, Marc called back. I took the phone and went to the kitchen so my daughter would not hear me, in case I had to raise my voice.

"I apologize," he said and hung up.

16

"LET'S START LOOKING FOR HOUSES in the Winston Salem area," Sam suggested. There were websites online where a person could search for real estate listings. I thought it was a great idea because he was going to retire in two years.

"Sure. What kind of house would you like? A three-bedroom?" I asked.

"No, I was thinking of something bigger. Something with an in-law suite in the basement so my pops can move in. He doesn't need that big house, and he's been talking about putting it on the market for years now. I think if we found something like that, it would motivate him to go on and sell it. The taxes on that house are ridiculous!"

The next day, I started looking at houses online that had a full apartment in the basement with a separate entrance. There weren't that many, but there were some. I saved them on the computer so that I could show them to Sam when he had time to look at them. He had also found some.

"When are we going to start on that baby?" I asked.

"What about tonight?" he joked.

"I'm serious!" I said, trying to pull away from him, tickling me. I didn't want to be thirty-five-years-old and pregnant.

"I'm serious. Let's start tonight?"

"We can pretend tonight, but my ovulation date is not for another three weeks," I said, cuddling up to him.

Over the next few months, we worked hard trying to get pregnant, and each month I got my period.

"I think we're trying too hard," I said, after six months.

"You're right. Let's just forget about it, and if and when it happens, it happens."

We stopped looking at the calendar, just relaxed, and enjoyed each other, as we did before. The following April, I got pregnant! I was excited. We had also found a few more houses we wanted to check out.

Sam flew to Winston Salem to see the houses. I made him promise to take videos of the houses while the agent showed him each one. Unfortunately, we didn't agree on any of them that trip, so it was back to the drawing board. I knew we had to find something soon because now, he only had ten more months in the military.

I waited until I was five months pregnant before I told Jazmine she was going to have a little sister or brother. I had no choice. By then, I was showing. She was excited! She was going to be a big sister.

"What would you like to have, a baby brother or baby sister?" I asked.

"I think I would like a baby brother," she answered.

"Really? Why a brother?" I just knew she would want a little sister.

"Boys are easier to boss around than girls!" she said, laughing.

That's what she thought!

I started back looking at houses online and finally found three more I liked. Once again, Sam flew out to Winston Salem and videotaped the houses while the agent showed him around. The last house he was shown was in the Country Club area of Winston Salem. It had an in-law suite that had a private entrance, two bedrooms, a living room, a beautiful kitchen, and two bathrooms. The upstairs had four bedrooms, three and one-half bathrooms, a den, a huge kitchen, and a sunroom. I loved it!

Sam started the paperwork on the house. When it was time to close on the house, he made one more trip out there.

When he returned to Texas, we discussed me moving now before I got so big that I could not fly any longer.

While school was dismissed for the summer, Jazmine and I went to North Carolina. All of our household items were packed and shipped to Winston Salem, and Sam moved into the officer's quarters.

Big Sam picked us up at the airport. "You know you took a chance flying, right? If they knew you were seven months pregnant, you wouldn't have gotten onto that plane," he said as we waited for our luggage.

Big Sam had the For Sale in his yard. As we entered the driveway, I saw him looking at it sadly. I knew it was hard for him to let go of this house, but one person didn't need a six-bedroom house. Sam didn't want to move us into the house because he said it held too many sad memories for him. We all needed a fresh start.

Big Sam hired a contractor to make repairs and to bring the house up to date. Jazmine and I were going to spend the night with him at his house, and the next day, we were going to meet the movers at our house and get things unpacked and organized. Big Sam was getting his things packed up from his house and moved into the basement.

While he was moving in downstairs, we were moving in upstairs. I was seven months pregnant; there wasn't much I could do except boss everyone around, and I enjoyed every minute of that. Even then, it took three weeks before the house was set up like I wanted it to be.

Sam finally joined us in Winston Salem, now almost fully retired and ready to move on with the next phase of our lives. He had a few loose ends he had to tie up in Killeen.

When I went to pick him up from the airport, it was good seeing him rushing toward me. I had a lot of work for him to do; mainly, getting the nursery organized for our son's arrival.

Sam was in bed, sleeping, and I was taking a shower. I felt the first sharp labor pain, dried off, and while I was doing that, my water broke. I could hardly believe it was happening like this.

With Jazmine, I wasn't sure if I was really in labor. I had gone back and forth several times because I thought I was in labor but wasn't. This time, boom!

I shook Sam gently.

"Sam, I need to go to the hospital; my water broke."

He half-opened his eyes.

"What?" he asked and turned over.

"Sam, my water broke."

He jumped up this time and had me sit down. He ran to the closet, pulled on his jeans, and pulled a shirt over his head.

"Put your shoes on, Sam. Relax! I have to get dressed."

I got dressed and buzzed downstairs for Big Sam to let him know the baby was coming. We woke up Jazmine, and we all went to the hospital. We called my dad from the car to tell him that I was on my way to the hospital to have the baby.

"Call me when he comes here!" Daddy said, sounding excited.

An hour later, our son, Samuel III, was born.

Everyone agreed we would call him Iketa, which is Yoruba for Third.

He was a beautiful baby! He came into the world weighing eight pounds ten ounces, twenty-one inches long. He had a headful of curly hair and dimples, like Sam and his father.

After Big Sam and Jazmine had gone home, Sam and I were left to admire our son.

"Look at those big hands! He's going to be a football player," he said proudly.

"I don't care what he decides to be, as long as he is good at it," I said proudly admiring his long fingers and thinking he would be a pianist.

"You did good, baby."

"We did good!"

I was tired; I dozed off and left Sam holding our son and smiling. When I opened my eyes a couple of hours later, he was still holding him. I took a nice warm shower, cleaned up, and came back to bed. He was still holding the baby.

"You know, you can go home tomorrow, if you like," the nurse said. I didn't like hospitals. I gladly went home the next day.

While I was in the hospital, Big Sam, Sam, and Jazmine got the nursery looking beautiful. Blue and white balloons were floating against the ceiling; fresh flowers were in my bedroom, the living room, and the kitchen.

17

WHEN I GOT HOME, I WENT straight to bed. I was drained. The first night, I woke up only to breastfeed and take a shower. The next morning, I was feeling much better. I was able to get up and go downstairs, where the family was staring at the baby, and waiting for someone to fix breakfast.

I put on a pot of coffee and took down a couple of boxes of cold cereal.

"Come on, guys, breakfast!" I called. They looked a bit disappointed to see a box of Cap'n Crunch and Cheerios on the table, beside a gallon of milk. However, they didn't complain. While they were getting their breakfast, I sat down by Iketa's bassinet and talked to him. His eyes were wide open, and he looked intently at me as I spoke as if he could understand what I was saying.

"What do you think about all of these people staring at you all the time? Are you sick of it yet?" I asked. To my surprise, he smiled.

"Did you notice how alert he is?" I asked Big Sam, who was leaning in to look at him.

"When Sammy was born, his eyes were closed for at least two or three days. Now babies are born looking around. You would think they have been here before," he said.

"Do you want some coffee, hon?" Sam asked.

I wanted a cup so badly, but with breastfeeding the baby, I couldn't have any coffee; I couldn't have any tea, either.

"I can't have any. But you know what would be good? A cold glass of milk." I was sarcastic because I hated milk. Yet, it was the only thing I could drink right now, besides juice.

After the baby went to sleep that evening, Sam and I cuddled. He was going to be leaving to go back to Texas the next evening. He only had two more weeks left to transition out of the military before returning home. I could already tell those two weeks were going to drag by slowly.

"Will you be ready for some loving by the time I return?" he asked.

"I'll be ready, but not my body. You know we have to wait six weeks!"

"Six weeks! Why?" he asked, sounding serious.

"Because I have to heal, silly! A whole human came out of me!"
I said, laughing.

"And a whole human wants to go inside you!"

"Why don't you go down and spend some time with your
father.
I'm going to take a nap while the baby is sleeping."

He kissed me on the forehead.

"Good night, beautiful!"

Three hours later, Iketa's crying woke me up. I held him in my
arms, fed him, and hummed to him while he enjoyed his dinner.
He stared up at me the entire time. I wondered what he was
thinking. A couple of times, I asked him that question.

"What is it that you want to tell me? I can tell you want to say
something. What is it?"

When he was done eating, I held him against my shoulder to
burp him. Sam came in, just as I was about to change his diaper.

"Let me do it!" he said.

"You want to change his diaper? You know he made a stinky?" I said.

"I'm going to be away for two weeks. I don't want him to forget who I am."

Before Sam even finished changing him, I had fallen asleep. Each time I woke up, he was holding the baby, who was staring up into his face. I knew Sam was going to be an excellent father to our son because of how he was with Jazmine.

The next morning, I called Daddy to see when he was coming down.

"I will be down for the party," he said.

We had planned a family dinner for when Sam retired.

"Okay. I miss you, but I can wait two weeks," I said.

After speaking to Jazmine, Sam, and Big Sam, we said our goodbyes until the end of the month.

Sam was going to be leaving at nine that night, heading to the airport in Greensboro. I told him he needed to try to get a nap before he had to leave, but all he wanted to do was spend time with the baby and Jazmine.

I packed a sandwich and some fruit for him to eat on the flight since meals were not served on the red-eye flights.

At 6:30, I told him again he needed to take a nap, but he insisted that he was fine.

He dressed in his uniform, kissed, hugged all of us goodbye, and he and Big Sam left for the airport.

"Call me when you get back to the base," I said. Jazmine and I stood in the doorway, waving goodbye as they backed out of the driveway.

I cleaned up the kitchen and put the leftover food away. I took a shower and was just settling in when Big Sam came home from the airport.

"Sammy got off good. He should be back at the base by six a.m. You get some rest. If you need anything, buzz me," he said.

"Okay, Pops. Have a good night," I said.

I woke up a couple of times to feed the baby and change him. The last time, I tried to stay awake so that I wouldn't miss Sam's phone call. While I waited, I started reading a book I had been trying to read for a month. I glanced at the clock, and it was nearly seven.

161

I wondered why he hadn't called yet, so I called him. It went straight to voicemail. I went downstairs, got a glass of juice, and went back to our bedroom.

By eight, I had left him several messages. I had a horrible feeling something wasn't right. I called Big Sam. "I haven't heard from Sam yet. I'm worried." "He'll call. You know Sammy," he said.

That was why I was concerned because I knew Sam. Sam would have called as soon as he stepped off of that plane. Something was not right. I decided to call the airline and see if there had been any delays with his flight.

There hadn't been. So, where was Sam?

I had nervous energy and went downstairs to make breakfast. Jazmine was watching TV; the baby slept in his bassinet. I called for Big Sam to come upstairs and get some food, and I went to take a shower.

I was just putting on my clothes when I heard the doorbell. It was almost 11 a.m. Jazmine came to the bedroom door to tell me that someone was at the door to see me.

"Who is it?" I asked.

"Two men in uniforms," she replied.

I walked downstairs with my heart beating so loudly that I could hear it. When I saw the two Army officers, I knew what they wanted.

"Go away! Don't you dare say it! I just had a baby! Don't you dare!" I screamed.

They stepped into the foyer and removed their hats.

"Mrs. Stewart, we are sorry to have to tell you ..."

"No! No! Don't you dare!" I screamed again.

Big Sam appeared, "What's going on up here?" he asked and then saw the officers.

"Oh, Lord," he whispered.

"There was a car accident this morning, and Captain Stewart was seriously injured. He was transported to the hospital, where he later passed away," he said.

I broke free from my father-in-law, and I grabbed that officer. "Please, tell me you made a mistake! Please! We just had a baby!"

When I came to, I was lying on the couch. Jazmine was crying and fanning me. I sat up and looked around the room. The officers were gone, and there was no one there but Big Sam. He was crying and shaking his head.

"I can't believe this! I can't believe this!" he kept saying.

Sam was his only son. He was my husband. He was the father of my children. And now he was gone.

My father flew down that day and stayed with my children while I flew to Texas with Big Sam to identify and claim my husband's remains. I cried all the way to Texas. I knew I had to pull it together to get through this.

We caught a taxi to the hospital. Big Sam did all of the talking; I stared straight ahead, wearing dark shades and clutching his arm. Major Anderson led us to the elevator, and we rode it down to the morgue. We walked down a long corridor and turned a corner. He stopped at the door.

"Captain Stewart sustained trauma to his head and face. If you don't want to Mrs. Stewart, his father can identify the body," he said. I gasped and felt myself getting weak.

"My son has a tattoo on his left forearm that says Emma and has roses around the name. Can you just show me that?" he asked.

"Yes, sir!" he said.

I waited in the hallway, listening to their footsteps as they walked across the tiled floor. I heard the door open to the drawer where my husband's remains were.

Big Sam must have changed his mind because I heard him let out a gut-wrenching moan. I leaned against the wall to keep from falling. I looked at the second hand on my watch ticking.

Six seconds later, I heard their footsteps as they made their way across the floor, and the door opened. Big Sam stepped into the hallway and held out his arms for me. I embraced him.

I know that must have been difficult for him.

"Let's go," he said.

We went back upstairs with the Major and filled out the paperwork to have his body accompany us on the flight back to Winston Salem. I don't think either of us said anything until we were in North Carolina. He parked the car in the garage. He went to his apartment downstairs, and I went upstairs. My father was waiting at the door, holding the baby.

I hadn't noticed my breasts were leaking milk. I went to my bedroom, changed clothes, and got a breast pump. Jazmine came in, carrying the baby. "Here, Mommy, feed him," she said.

I didn't want to breastfeed him. I didn't even want to hold him right now. I gave her the bottle with the breast milk in it. "Please feed him." I pulled my bra back over my breast, and I laid down to go to sleep.

I didn't want to see the baby right then. Big Sam and Daddy had to make the arrangements for the funeral. I couldn't do it. I didn't want to do it.

Mommy flew up that night. It was the first time she and Daddy had seen each other in over twenty-four years. While I cried, she came to lay in the bed with me and held me in her arms.

"Baby, I know this is probably going to be the worst thing you will ever have to deal with. But you have to get up because you have these babies depending on you. You have to get up," she said.

I knew she was right; my children needed me.

I took a shower and got dressed. I didn't know there were so many people at the house until I went to the kitchen. I didn't even know any of them, but they were members of Sam's family, friends, and his frat brothers. Each of them came to hug me and tell me how much Sam meant to them. They apologized and extended their condolences for my loss. I thanked them and moved to the next person.

Two days later, I sat on the front row, right in front of my husband's casket covered in the flag, and listened to his friends and colleagues talk about what a wonderful soldier, son, father, husband, and friend he was. I rocked back and forth, holding my daughter's hand, leaning against my mother's shoulder, and seeing the worried looked on Big Sam's face.

I don't know how we did it, but we made it out of bed each day. We ate. We showered. We breathed. And the days turned into weeks and the weeks into months and the months into years.

My mother flew back to Texas and promised she would come back soon and have more time to spend with me. After a couple of weeks, Daddy went back to New York. Big Sam began closing the door that led downstairs to his apartment. He was avoiding me, not even coming up to get breakfast with us anymore. I told

Jazmine to give him some time. I also felt bad for her because now she had lost two fathers.

My poor baby would never know his father at all. That hurt me more than anything.

I would wake up sometimes in a cold sweat, hoping and praying that this had all been a bad dream. But it wasn't, and I had to accept that. I had to be strong for my children. Sam wouldn't want me to crumble.

18

ONE OF THE CLAUSES IN THE insurance policy paid off the house in the event of the death of either Sam or me. Since he had already filled out his retirement papers and was legally retired, I was able to get his pension and the widow's benefits. We were going to be fine financially, but I needed to get a job.

I needed it to allow me something to do with my time. I was sick of sitting around the house, feeling sorry for myself. I began applying for jobs online.

Each time someone called for an interview, I would go and hope someone called me for a second interview or offered me the job. But the months went by without a callback.

I saw a job online for a position at the library and applied. It wasn't what I wanted to do, but I had to get out of this house. The baby was now two years old. I hadn't called his name since his father died. I simply called him the baby. I just couldn't bring myself to call him the Third again, no matter the language. I knew

I couldn't call him the baby forever. One day, I decided I was going to call him Little Sam.

I was planting flowers the day the director of the library called for an interview. She told me she had met me before at an event I had attended. I didn't remember her, but that didn't mean anything. I had been going to things with Big Sam for a year, totally in automatic pilot.

He seemed to know everyone in Winston-Salem. When he got sick of me sitting around, feeling sorry for myself, he took me where he went.

On the day of the interview, Big Sam and Little Sam were hanging out together. I put on a yellow dress and put my hair in a bun. I changed purses and headed to the library.

My interview was with the assistant director, Mrs. Howard, the manager of the department, Mr. Fields, where the open position was, and his manager, Mary.

I sat across from Mr. Fields and Mary, with Mrs. Howard on my right. Each of them interviewed me. I answered their questions to the best of my ability.

The job was with the Smart Start program, which was a new division of the library. The Smart Start program was an outreach program. There were two bookmobiles. One would service the Hispanic community by bringing them books, puppets, and tapes. Spanish speaking storytellers would share stories with the children at the two community centers that catered to their needs. The other bookmobile would service the African American community and anyone else who lived in their neighborhood. Several community centers catered to the African American and Hispanic communities. A mini-library would be housed at the centers. Children could check out books and tapes from the mini library, or they could check them out from the bookmobile. Storytellers would service both the community centers and the bookmobiles.

There was a lot of work to do to process the thousands of books that came in for the bookmobiles and the community centers.

When I was offered the job, I accepted it because it sounded like not just a necessity, but also exciting. "It will certainly keep me busy," I thought.

I started calling around, interviewing for someone to watch Little Sam, when Big Sam offered to watch him.

"Are you sure?" I asked.
"Of course, I'm sure. This is my buddy!" he said, smiling.

On the first day on the job, my eleven coworkers and I met in the conference room to have a meet and greet. There was a breakfast buffet available and a coffee bar. I got to meet all of my coworkers that day.

Most of the ladies had been working together for years, and they all knew each other. Another woman named Rhonda, a young man named Jamel, and I were the "new kids on the block" because we had never worked at the library.

The other ladies had programs they were already responsible for. So, it left Rhonda, Jamel, and I in charge of entering the books into the library system and processing them for checkout. Midway through the entering process, a new development happened. The library decided they would begin servicing certain daycare centers that were already getting services from the library through the storytellers.

Now we had to put together Storytime kits. Each kit would contain a picture book, puzzles, puppets, and flashcards about that story. That was time-consuming. I would get home mentally exhausted every day.

I thanked God every day for Big Sam. I didn't know how I would have been able to carry this load without him.

19

ONE DAY AT WORK, MY PHONE rang. "Good morning, Smart Start," I said.

"May I speak to Mrs. Stewart?" said a familiar voice.

"Wayne? Wayne!" I squealed, excited to hear from him. I hadn't spoken to Wayne since I had left Hampton twelve years ago.

"I've been looking all over for you! I finally tracked down Marc. He acted like he didn't want to give me your digits, but he told me you had gotten married to this captain in the Army. So, I tracked him down. I'm sorry for your loss."

"No, it's okay. It is so good to hear your voice. How are you and the family?"

"Well, I'm good. Sherita and I aren't together anymore. We've been divorced for about five years. Yeah! I live in Atlanta now."

"I'm sorry to hear that."

"Well, you know me. I gave it my best, and it wasn't good enough. I know you're at work. So, take down my number and call me tonight when you get home."

I wrote his number down! Yeah, my days of trying to remember numbers were over.

The day dragged on and on. I could hardly wait until things were quiet around the house, and I could actually call Wayne and talk without a two-year-old running around.

After dinner, I cleaned the kitchen. As usual, Little Sam slid his fat butt down the stairs to hang out with his grandpa.

I went over Jazmine's homework, and we lay across the bed, watching her favorite show until it was her bedtime.

"Good night, Ma," she said and kissed me on the cheek.

"Good night, baby."

She took her shower and went to bed.

I got a glass of wine and called Wayne.

"What happened with you and Sherita?" I asked.

"We just grew apart, that's all. Now let me ask you. What happened to you and my boy, Kevin?"

"I was supposed to return to Hampton. He gave me his phone number, and I didn't have anything to write it down with. But you know, I'm good with remembering numbers. I told him I would remember it. But when I got back to New York, Jazmine was sick. The military sent us to San Antonio, Texas. I called Sherita so many times; I lost track of how many. I left her messages on top of messages to give to Kevin. I even told her to tell you to call me. She told me that Kevin was no good. He had hurt a lot of her other friends. He had a new girlfriend."

"What? What? Are you serious? She never gave Kevin any of your messages. That boy was messed up for a long time because he never heard back from you."

"Are you serious?"

"Yeah, I'm serious. I had to nurse him back to health after almost a year. He finally gave up. But he had never dated any of her friends! Nobody! Why the hell did she tell you that?"

I had an idea, but I wasn't going to tell him. I loved Wayne like a brother. I wasn't going to hurt him like that.

"I can give you his number; he would love to hear from you."

"No, I'm not ready to talk to anyone right now."

"Oh, yeah. I'm sorry; that was insensitive of me."

176

We caught up on some of the things that happened to me; the good, the bad, and the painful. We promised to stay in touch, and we said our goodbyes.

That night, I thought about Kevin, but I wasn't ready to talk to him. I wouldn't even know what to say after all of these years. I just couldn't talk to him right now.

20

I LOVED MY JOB! EVERY DAY I got to meet some awesome youngsters. I was glad I had accepted this position. I loved my coworkers! We were making a difference in our community.

We were like a big family. Rhonda, Jamel, and I spent time together away from the job. She and I went to brunch together. He and I played tennis together. They both liked poetry; we often got together and attended one of the poetry events around town.

One Friday after I got off from work, Big Sam invited me to a formal event at the Stevens Center that upcoming Saturday night. I hadn't been to a formal event since I had Little Sam. I needed a break, so I agreed to go with him.

I went to a salon that Saturday morning to get my hair done. At seven, I lay a black strapless gown on the bed. I took a nice hot bath and got ready to go. "It's going to be a perfect evening," I thought. Big Sam told me that he was going to be driving his Bentley. He had taken it to get serviced earlier in the week.

When he came up to get me, he looked handsome in his black tux.

Big Sam held the door open and helped me get in. When we pulled up in front of the theatre, I felt like a zillion dollars! All eyes were on us. I should say they were all on him. All of the ladies were eyeing my father-in-law. He was a handsome and dignified man.

"Don't you dare leave me alone tonight! I see an old girlfriend," he whispered.

"I will try my best," I said, chuckling.

I saw people there I knew also. Every step I took, Big Sam was right beside me, holding on to my arm. I wanted to see this woman causing him to act this way.

"Pops, where is the old girlfriend?" I asked.

"Do you see that woman with the short red dress on? That's her! We only went out a few times, but she got her nose wide open," he said.

"Stop it! She's looking at you. Go say hi and stop being silly." I stepped away before he had a chance to get my arm.

When I saw Short Red Dress approaching Big Sam, I was on the other side of the room. He looked so uncomfortable that I had to smile.

"Hi, Rhonda! How come you didn't tell me you were coming out tonight?" I asked.

"I wasn't planning to. My Dad backed out, and my mom didn't want the extra ticket to go to waste, so here I am. Girl, I would rather be eating some chicken wings and pork fried rice than to be here with these uppity folks," she said.

"Look at my father-in-law! He is so funny!" I said. From where we were standing, I could see he was backed against the wall, and she had him cornered.

Even though it was a bit funny, I could see how uncomfortable he was and decided to go to his rescue.

I excused myself and went back to him. I hooked my arm into his and walked away with him in tow. I didn't appreciate women like this. This was the type of woman who had broken up my first marriage. They made me sick!

"Thanks for saving me. It's hard to be polite when women come off like that, and I was just about to lose it," he said.

180

The lights dimmed three times, letting us know the show was about to start. We went inside the theatre and took our seats. I hadn't seen a play in a long time, and this was just as exciting as the others I had seen. As we were leaving the theatre, Short Red Dress was waiting by the door. As we went through the door, she gave him a piece of paper she had written her phone number on. He took it, and when we were outside, he put it in the ashtray holders at the curb. She hadn't seen him do it because she blew him a kiss as we waited for the valet to bring the car around.

On the way home, I wanted to know the story of Short Red Dress and him.

"She was married to a colleague of mine about twenty-five years ago. He passed away about ten years ago. I was at an event, and she came over to talk to me. She was so aggressive that when she asked me out, I told her no, but she kept on asking, insisting that I go with her to whatever it was. I can't even remember what it was; art show, poetry, play, I don't remember. She spent the entire night acting like an octopus. She was all hands. I took her back to her place, and she invited me to come inside. I went in, and well, we ended up in bed, and I couldn't get out of there fast enough. After that, she showed up everywhere I went because we were in the same circle of friends. She does this every time I see her."

"Wow! I didn't know older ladies acted like that, too."

"Well, they do. I'm old school. I like to be the one pursuing a woman, not the other way around. It doesn't seem natural to me, that's all I'm saying."

I understood what he was telling me. I think I would have felt the same way if I were a man. "Would you like a nightcap?" I asked once we got inside the house. "I'll take a raincheck. I'm tired and just want to get out of these stuffy clothes and hit the sack. Sleep tight. See you in the morning," he said and went downstairs. A few seconds later, he called me.

"Come see this!" he said. I went down to his apartment to see my son lying on his couch, the TV on, a jar of peanut butter with a knife in it was on the coffee table, and slices of bread all over the floor. His tired little two-year-old butt was covered in peanut butter, and he was knocked out!

"Go on to bed. I'll clean him up. He can stay down here tonight," he said.

an affiliate of the nationals. Each year, I attended the festival, no matter where it was. Then I got word the next festival was going to be held in Atlanta. I called Wayne to let him know I was going to be in Atlanta that November, and we needed to get together.

He was just as excited to see me as I was to see him. We hadn't seen each other in seventeen years. Jazmine was a freshman at Winston Salem State University. Iketa was a very tall twelve-year-old who loved track, basketball, and programming computers.

Instead of Big Sam looking after them, they were now looking after him. He had slowed down a little bit in the past ten years as he was pushing seventy-five.

I tried to get all of them involved in storytelling, but they were not interested in being storytellers. They liked to hear stories and attended some of the events I attended. So, I usually went to festivals with Stella.

After the festival in Philly, Rhonda never went to another festival. It wasn't that she didn't enjoy the festival; she had a bad experience with one of our co-workers and decided it was best to distance herself from that particular coworker. She

Stella, two other storytellers, and I drove to Atlanta that year. As soon as I checked into the hotel, I called Wayne. I was excited to see him, but he was at work. He told me that he would be by at 6:30. I started getting ready at 5:30. I knew from experience that Wayne was prompt. By the time he called me from the lobby, I was in the elevator going down, anyway. When the doors to the elevator opened, I met him in front of the hotel.

As soon as I saw Wayne, I squealed with delight.

"You haven't changed a bit!" he said.

I had, but I appreciated him being kind. He looked the same too, except for the few strands of gray hair in his mustache.

We went to dinner at Pompadours. Over drinks and appetizers, we talked about the old days, the people we knew, and where they were now. And, of course, we talked again about Kevin.

"I talked to him the same night you and I talked. He couldn't believe I had found you. He's still single. I think the brother is waiting on you," he said.

"Really? He's never gotten married?"

"No, he hasn't gotten married. So, tell me about your husband. Where did you two meet? How did he pass away?"

"I met him a couple of years after I moved to Texas. My mom introduced us. He retired from the Army but had some loose ends to fix before joining us in Winston Salem. My husband died three days after I gave birth to our son. He had come to North Carolina for the birth. He wouldn't get any sleep because he wanted to be up for everything the baby needed. The night he flew back to Texas, he had to drive from the airport in Dallas back to Killeen. He fell asleep at the wheel, they think, and crashed the car. He was only seven miles from Killeen when he was killed."

"Oh, hon! I'm sorry. I know that must have been very difficult."

"It's okay. We had just purchased a home there. His dad lives in the basement apartment. The kids and I live in the main part of the house. We are all very close."

"How long ago was this?"

"Twelve years ago."

"You haven't thought about getting married again?"

"Maybe I'm waiting on Kevin," I said and smiled.

After dinner, he dropped me back off at the hotel. I invited him to come to at least one of the events that week. He promised me that he would try, but Wayne never showed up.

We talked on the phone once again before I left heading back to Winston Salem. We promised that we would stay in touch.

A few days later, I came home from work tired from a long day and was sitting on the bed, trying to muster up the energy to get undressed and fix something for dinner. My son came in to let me know that someone named Kevin had called earlier.

Whatever tiredness I was feeling, was now gone. I took the piece of paper he was holding out to me with Kevin's number scribbled down on it, and I held it to my chest. I looked at the number and realized it was the same number he had given me many years ago in Hampton; 757-621-1341!

I repeated the number over and over out loud and began laughing. Now I would remember it! I couldn't stop myself from laughing.

"Mommy, what are you laughing about?" my son asked. I motioned for him to come over, and I hugged him.

"Mommy is just happy, baby. Go on back downstairs; I'll be down in a few minutes to start dinner."

I changed clothes and went down to make a quick dinner. I went to the basement door to ask Big Sam if he wanted anything to eat. He let me know he was cooking because he had a lady friend coming over. I closed the door, leaving him at it.

I wasn't hungry now that I had Kevin's number. After I fixed my child's plate, I excused myself and went back upstairs to call Kevin. It was after seven. I figured he would be home from work. I dialed the number and waited for it to ring with my heart beating loudly.

"Hello," he said.

"Is this Kevin?" I asked, even though I knew it was him.

"Yes, this is Kevin. Wow! How are you? You're like, eighteen years late with this call," he said, laughing.

"How do you know my voice?"

"I'll never forget your voice. How have you been?"

"I am okay. Kevin, I am so sorry."

"Sorry about what? You know that was a long time ago. We don't even have to go back to that time. What have you been up to? What's going on?"

"I'm going to be in Hampton for a conference on the 19th of November. I was hoping that you would like to see me."

"You're coming to Hampton? Great, sure, I would love to see you. I wish I could stay and talk, but I have a meeting I have to get to. Let me give you my email address, and you can just email me the details. Write it down, okay?" He laughed.

"Oh, okay. Give it to me."

He gave me his email address and thanked me for calling him back. Then he was gone, just like that! He didn't match my excitement at all. I was hurt and called Wayne.

"He acted like he didn't even want to talk to me again. He gave me his email address! I wanted to tell him what happened, so he didn't think that I was using him or didn't care about him," I whined.

"Maybe you caught him off guard. Or, maybe he did have a meeting he had to get to. Come on, babe. Don't be trying to read something that isn't there. Relax! It's been how many years since you last talked to him? What? Seventeen or eighteen? Relax. Let him get over the initial shock of it all. I was shocked when I heard your voice, and I ain't ever been with you like that. Okay. Chill!"

"Okay. I guess I thought we would talk for a couple of hours or so. I don't know; maybe I am making a big deal about it. It was just so good to hear his voice, Wayne." "What did he do to you?" He laughed.

"He loved me like no one ever had. He also laid it on me!" I said, laughing.

"I figured as much! But look, babe, just chill. Send him the particulars for your trip and go and have a good time. Write down the number this time. I haven't had dinner yet, so I'll holler at you later."

After he hung up, I wrote Kevin's phone number down in my address book and put it in my nightstand drawer. I lay on the bed and tried to remember our time together. For the life of me, I could not remember the details. I needed some wine.

I went downstairs and poured me a big glass of wine, not in a wineglass but a mason jar. I sipped it, waiting for the tub to fill up for my bubble bath.

While I sat in hot water with bubbles up to my neck, I replayed the conversation with Kevin. Was I wanting more because I was lonely? Or was I just reading too much into it, as Wayne said? I hadn't been on a date or in a man's arms since my husband passed away thirteen years ago. That was a long time.

The next day at work, I was telling Rhonda about my call to Kevin.

"Girl, maybe he did have a meeting to go to! Don't start acting like a diva! Besides, you probably caught him off guard. Relax!"

The festival was nearly four months away. I had plenty of time to relax.

I emailed Kevin the details of the trip, which hotel I was going to be staying at, the time I would be arriving at Hampton, and leaving. I got no response from him, but I had to assume he had gotten the email.

I tried to relax and let it go. I picked up the phone to call him at least twenty times in the months before the festival. I wanted him to be as excited to hear from me as I was to finally, after all of these years, get his phone number.

I never heard from him, and I was truly disheartened.

22

WHEN RHONDA AND I WERE PREPARING for our trip to Hampton, she told me over and over to just relax, and what will be will be, and other philosophical musings. I wanted Kevin in my life.

We decided we would be driving up to Hampton and would get on the road at noon. I had washed and filled the car with gas the day before. When I went to pick her up, she asked, "Have you heard anything from Kevin?"

"Nope! Not a word. I only assume he got my email."

"Why didn't you call him this morning to remind him?"

"Because I didn't want to seem desperate. Remember, you said to relax and what will be will be. So, I'm working on that."

"Call him now and let him know, real nonchalant like Let him know that you are getting on the road and hope to see him while you're in Hampton. Just say it like that. Like if you do, you do. And if you don't, so what! Call him!"

While she was putting her things in the trunk, I called him.

"Hello."

"Hi, Kevin. How are you?"

"Hey! I'm doing good. How about you?"

"I was just calling to let you know that I'm getting ready to hit the highway. I hope to see you while I'm there if you are not busy."

"I was going to shoot over there this evening after I got off work. So, you're driving up? Drive safe. I'll talk to you later," he said as if he were busy, and I had interrupted him.

"Oh, okay. See you later."

Why was he always rushing me off the phone? Dang!

"Relax! Relate! Release!" Rhonda teased.

Rhonda and I had traveled by car before. I knew before we even made it to the highway, she would be sleeping, and this trip was no different. I turned on the radio and got us to Hampton that afternoon around 4:30.

196

We checked into our rooms and went to get something to eat at a nearby soul food café. Since Kevin said he was coming by after work, I ordered my food to go and rushed back to the hotel. That way, I could eat, take a quick shower, and lay out the clothes I was going to wear to see him.

I got comfortable and took a nice nap, setting the alarm to wake me up at six.

The ringing phone woke me up. I answered it without looking to see who it was.

"Hey! It's Kevin. I'm parking the car and about to walk to your hotel."

"Okay. I just woke up. I'll be down in a few minutes."

I rushed to the bathroom, brushed my teeth, and pulled on a pair of jeans and a white blouse. I finger-combed my natural and put on some lipstick. I slipped on my black pumps and grabbed my purse.

When I stepped off the elevator, Kevin was sitting in a chair near the window. He stood up and walked toward me, smiling. I wanted to run into his arms, but I followed his lead. He hugged me gently and quickly.

I invited him to sit down where there were two chairs together. Many of my storytelling friends were checking into the hotel and kept interrupting us to speak and hug me. Each time I returned to where Kevin was sitting, he was checking his watch.

"I apologize for that. We only get to see each other once a year at this event. You look good, Kevin!"

He had some gray hair at his temples, and a few laugh lines, but he looked the same. The twinkle was still in his eyes, however, he looked nervous and anxious. I felt that any minute he was going to leap from the seat and make a dash for whatever was waiting for him.

"You do, too. You filled out a bit, but it looks good on you. I like your hair," he said and chuckled. I tried to remember how I wore my hair when he saw me twenty-some years ago. I probably had a relaxer. Now, I wore a big bushy wild natural, or what we used to call an afro. He reached out and touched it.

"It's all mine," I said, laughing.

"You had a lot of hair back then, too," he said. He reached into his jacket and removed a photo of me, sitting on the beach in Norfolk with the wind blowing through my hair.

I took the picture and looked at it. I remembered when he took this. I was surprised he still had it.

"Give it back to me," he said.

I handed it back, and he put it back in his pocket. He said something else, but there was so much noise in the lobby now, I couldn't hear what he said.

"Would you like to go into the bar, it may be a bit quieter in there," I suggested. He held the door for me to enter, and we took seats at the bar.

"What can I get you two?" the bartender asked.

"Can I get a white wine?" he responded. Turning toward me, he asked, "Would you like something?"

"Can I have a Chivas on the rocks with a twist of lemon?"

"Oh, yeah, I remember that is your drink of choice. Look at you!" he said and laughed. I had something I wanted to get off my chest, and I finally had the opportunity.

"Kevin, when I left Hampton that day, it was my intention ..." I started to say, but he cut me off.

"You don't have to explain. That was forever ago ..."

"I know. But I will feel so much better if I tell you what happened.
I got back to New York and ..."

"Really. It's not necessary."

"Okay. Okay. So, tell me what you've been up to the past several years," I said, giving up on telling him what happened for now.

"Just working. Paying the bills," he said, glancing at his watch again.

"Is there a game on? I noticed you keep checking your watch."

"I just had a long day at work, and I haven't eaten yet."

"I haven't eaten yet, either. Would you want to grab a bite here? I heard the food is very good."

"No, I'm going to cut out. Listen, it was nice seeing you." He picked up his glass of wine, gulped it down, and stood up.

It took me by surprise. "Okay. It was nice seeing you, too." I reached into my jeans pocket and removed the $1600 I felt I owed him.

"I want to give you this money back. I appreciate it ..."

"Please, keep it! That was a gift a long time ago. No strings attached." I swallowed the lump in my throat, and the tears I feared would erupt from me.

I drank my drink in one gulp and walked out of the bar with him. "Can I at least walk you to your car?" I asked.

"Sure, if you like."

I saw some of my storytelling friends and stopped to accept their hugs on the way out. Once outside, we walked to his car, which was parked several blocks away in silence. I wanted to say something, but I didn't know how to say the things I had wanted to say to him.

"It was good seeing you, Kevin," I said once we were beside his car. I wanted him to hug me again; to tell me he was glad he had come by to see me, or something.

"Yeah, same here."

I stood there shaking all over as he got in his car, made a U-turn, and drove away. I turned and walked back to the hotel alone. I went back to the bar, ordered another drink, and gulped it down.

After paying for it, I went upstairs and called Wayne.

"Hey! How did it go?" he asked.

"He was rude to me. He acted as if he saw me yesterday. He was here twenty-two minutes! I tried to explain what had happened, and he cut me off. I offered him his money, and he didn't want it. He doesn't care about me anymore. I wish I had never called him!" I said, crying.

"Hold on just a minute. No, let me call you right back. Hang tight."

I threw the phone down and fell across the bed, crying.

Twenty minutes later, Wayne called me back.

"That was Kevin. He was going on and on about how good you look. How much he wanted to kiss you; how the old feelings resurfaced. Now, what are you telling me? Cause these stories are not matching up!" he said.

"What? You're lying! He treated me like I was nothing to him! If he didn't want to see me, he should have just told me that!"

"I'm telling you! He said he wanted to … "

"Hold on, someone is calling me on the hotel phone."

"Hello?"

"What's your room number?" Kevin asked, sounding out of breath.

"611!"

"Wayne, that's Kevin! He's coming up to my room! I'll talk to you later!"

I went to the bathroom, wiped my tear-stained face, and put on more lipstick. I was now a little tipsy from gulping the Chivas, however, I was coherent enough that when he knocked, I wasn't standing there butt naked!

Before opening the door, I counted to three.

He stepped inside, and I locked the door.

"Can I kiss you?" he asked.

"You better!"

When he stopped kissing me, I was breathless.

"Kevin, please, I need to tell you what happened. Please, let me do that. It's important to me. I've been holding this in forever."

He sat down at the desk; I was sitting across from him on the edge of the bed. I told him exactly what happened, and he listened. I told him how my baby was sick when I returned to New York, and I took her to the ER right away. I tried to call him when I got back home, but I couldn't remember his phone number. I told him how I ended up in San Antonio and tried to call him again, and I finally called Sherita and told her to call him and give him my number. And how rude she was to me, and finally telling me that he was a terrible person, and had hurt several of her other friends. I told him how she told me he came to her house several times after I left and was with a different girl each time until he finally showed up with a big butt girl and said that she was his girlfriend.

"You are the first and only friend of Sherita's I have ever met. I don't know what she was talking about. She never told me that you called. And I never went to her house with a big butt girl."

"I figured that she was lying. I tried over the years to get friends of mine that worked for the military to find you, and I couldn't. I

204

loved you, Kevin, and I wanted to return to Hampton, I did. When I never heard from you, I decided to stay in Texas."

"When I didn't hear from you that night, I thought something had happened to you. I called Wayne's house, and Sherita answered the phone. She said she hadn't heard from you and didn't know how to contact you. I thought that was strange since y'all seemed to be close friends. I asked her a few times over the years about you, and she told me you had gotten married and was living in Texas. I was hurt about it. I loved you. I still love you," he said, rolling the chair closer to me.

"I did get married, but it was a few years after I left New York. My husband died in a car accident three days after I gave birth to our son. I had moved to North Carolina because he was retiring from the military. When he died, I was devastated, however, I had to put on my big girl bloomers and take care of my children. Years after he died, I reconnected with Wayne. That's how I found you."

Nineteen years had passed since the day I boarded the jet heading back to New York. I experienced a lot of things that shaped me into a different person. I was older, wiser, less prone to act on impulses. Everything about my life was different than what it was when I was a twenty-four-year-old woman who had been beaten up by life and the choices I had made.

What I wanted now, I could articulate, and in some cases, demand it. I wanted to spend the rest of my life with Kevin, and he wanted the same thing. We were both mature enough to know this time around was going to require work, commitment, sacrifices, and for us to get to know one another all over again.

We were willing to make that commitment to each other and to begin this journey, starting tonight. I didn't know how our story would end, but I knew I was excited about everything that would happen from this moment on.

THE END